DARK HAUNTINGS

BOOGER MCCLAIN OZARKS DETECTIVE SERIES BOOK 10

ALAN
BROWN

BRIAN
BROWN

This is a work of fiction. Names, characters, places, and incidents are products of the author's imagination or are used fictitiously and are not to be construed as real. Any resemblance to actual events, locations, organizations, or persons, living or dead, is entirely coincidental.

World Castle Publishing, LLC
Pensacola, Florida
Copyright © 2025 Alan Brown & Brian Brown
Hardback ISBN: 9798290448893
Paperback ISBN: 9798891264328
eBook ISBN: 9798891264335
First Edition World Castle Publishing, LLC, July 21, 2025
http://www.worldcastlepublishing.com

Licensing Notes

Cover: Cover Designs by Karen
Editor: Karen Fuller

CHAPTER ONE
THE DECISION

Standing at the foot of the bridge, Booger could hear Rose's thoughts as he prepared to cross.

"Don't leave me," Rose thought to herself. *"I don't want to go on without you."*

Booger steadied his feet and took a step towards the center. He knew he should have faith. On the other side of the bridge was everyone he ever loved, except Rose. *"In a blink of an eye, Rose will be here too. This is home."* Step, step, and another step.

"Booger!" Rose exclaimed. She was done thinking to herself. She was afraid. She was yelling. "I need you!"

Booger stopped dead in his tracks. "I don't think I can do this."

Mrs. Potts gave him a knowing smile. "Son, the choice is always yours, but you know you can."

That's when the man with the kangaroo tail stepped in. "You should turn back. Go save her. She needs you," he said as he mindlessly examined his fingernails.

"You don't have to listen to him, Buford. His job is to pull you away."

"But how can I go to heaven if I know she's struggling and in danger?"

"Rose is strong enough to help herself, Buford. Plus, you can help from the other side. Just like Nancy and your grandmother have helped you."

With tears in his eyes, he took another step. Then another.

"Booger! You damn fool! I need y-you," Rose said with her voice cracking at the end. She began crying.

"Rose!" Booger screamed. He couldn't help himself. The bridge of life shook at his exclamation.

"Go back," the man of the bridge said with a sneer. "She needs you."

"Buford, you've come too far. Remember what you've learned."

Booger was standing in the middle of the bridge. He knew that if he went back, there was no guarantee he'd be able to help his wife. What made the most sense was for him to press on, to cross the bridge, to be welcomed home. Still, his heart was torn in two. How could he deny her asking for help in her time of need?

Booger turned to Mrs. Potts. In that little classroom, she had prepared him for his journey to heaven. She had advocated for him even though his life on Earth did not warrant entrance past the Golden Gate.

"I can't help you, Buford," Mrs. Potts said in an empathetic voice. "*Free will*, remember? This has to be your choice."

The decision Booger would need to make was impossible. Leave his family and a place where he would spend eternity in a sort of utopia to join Rose back on Earth or leave Rose forever and join his family in Heaven. Could he risk his own eternal fate for Rose? Would she even want him to if she knew what he knows?

After being shot in that abandoned psych ward and lying in a coma on Earth, with his spirit stuck in a sort of purgatorian classroom somewhere on the edge of Heaven, Booger now had the opportunity to join his family and friends, to be in the presence of God, Jesus, and the Angels. He had the opportunity to fully

understand the meaning of life and to have all his questions
about God and Jesus answered. He would finally discover how
accurate the Bible really was. His life had been judged, and
despite his flaws, he was deemed worthy of admittance. This was
what all good Christians aspired to be when their spirit departed
their body.

But Booger was far from a good Christian. He couldn't
remember the last time he had been to a church. And, he had killed
before, several times before. In his 70-plus years, he had cussed,
lied, drank, and smoked too much. He had broken many of the
Ten Commandments. For Booger to get into Heaven was nothing
short of a miracle. There, he could spend eternity with Nancy, his
brother, and his parents. Booger had never stopped thinking of
his first wife and the wonderful life they built together. They had
dreamed of building a family and growing old together. Those
dreams were crushed when she died of cancer at such an early
age. He had loved her so much, and it had taken him so long to
get over her, to give himself fully to another wife. Now, she was
standing just ahead, waiting for him, smiling, holding out her
arms for him. She was even more beautiful than he remembered.
A few steps forward, and they could spend eternity together.

It seemed like a lifetime since he had seen Nancy. She was
his soulmate, his very first love, and for most of his life, she was
his only love. But in recent years, he had fallen in love again. Rose
was the other woman he had loved in his life. He had to make a
choice between spending eternity with Nancy or spending his
remaining lifetime with Rose. And he had to make that decision
now.

To look at his situation logically, there was only one clear
choice. By moving forward across that bridge, his afterlife would
be a utopia. Everyone he loved would be there; that is, everyone

but one. To turn away would mean spending the rest of his life with Rose, however long that might be, with no assurance that he would ever make it back to his family again. He would face the harsh realities of life again. Mankind was full of injustices, death, temptation, failures, greed, and pain. God had given man free will, and because of that, He had opened the door to Satan's temptations. Booger knew there were fates worse than death. He knew there was real evil in the world. He had seen it firsthand too many times to count. Life on Earth was a sort of purgatory, a waiting room for admittance to Hell or Heaven. And life on Earth, as Booger had experienced it, was a lot closer to Hell. He counted himself lucky to be able to return "home."

"Yes," Booger thought, "there was only one logical choice for him to make."

Just then, his eyes met the shining blue eyes of Nancy. She smiled at him, a knowing smile, and with an ocean of love in her eyes, she nodded her head. "It's okay, Booger. It's okay."

"What was OK?" he thought. *"Was Nancy saying everything would be OK if he just continued forward? Or, was his first love telling him that it would be OK to go back to Rose?"*

Suddenly, Nancy's smile was gone. A look of love and compassion filled her eyes. That was when Booger knew what Nancy meant.

Booger looked at the man with the kangaroo tail. Samuel, he was called. A fallen angel no longer accepted in the City. He would spend eternity outside the Golden Gates. Not evil, but not worthy of Heaven. Samuel had been assigned the task of taking souls not worthy of entering the Golden Gates back to Earth. Most were reincarnated, returning to Earth in whatever form God chose. They were sent there in an effort to make better choices with their lives. They were sent there with a clean slate, so to speak, an opportunity to please their Father in Heaven with their new life on Earth.

Others, like Booger, had their spirits prematurely leave their body. It wasn't their time, and they would be given free will to decide whether to stay or go back to Earth. Those souls would return to their same bodies to serve out their lives until God called them back.

Booger looked over at Samuel. There was no expression on his face. This would be Booger's decision.

The hospital room was eerily cold. A look of urgency was replaced with sorrow and disappointment. Booger McClain was dead. His heart flatlined for nearly five minutes. Rose refused to leave her husband's side. Doctors, nurses, and the entire code-red team worked to save Booger's life. But the electrical cardioversion had failed to bring him back to her. Three times, the doctor used the electric paddles, each time with more desperation. But it did not work.

An exhausted doctor, breathing heavily and sweating profusely, turned to his colleagues and said, "I'm going to call time of death."

"No," screamed Rose, grabbing the doctor's arm. "Please, I beg you, try one more time."

Rose dropped to the floor and prayed harder than she had ever prayed before. "Lord, I can't even remember the last time I asked you for anything. But please, Lord, grant me this one request, and I will never ask you for anything again. Bring my husband back to me."

The doctor, witnessing Rose's moving prayer, lifted the paddles one last time and dropped them on Booger's chest. As the electrical current jumped from the paddles into Booger's body, a beep began to appear on the heart monitor, soft and slow at first and then increasing in intensity. He was alive.

The hospital room, cold, eerily quiet just a few minutes earlier, was now warm and filled with happiness.

Rose jumped to her feet and ran to her husband's side, tears flowing down her cheeks as she grabbed his hand. He squeezed hers in return, gently at first and then with a strong grip as he opened his eyes for the first time in weeks.

"Rose," Booger whispered.

"I'm here," Rose replied through her tears.

"Rose?"

"Yes, sweetie."

"Can you get me a double cheeseburger? I'm starving."

"Damn it, Bufford T. McClain, you scared me to death."

CHAPTER TWO
ROAD TO RECOVERY

For the first time in over a month, Rose slept like a baby. Her husband was home. He'd beaten the odds and returned to life. But the road to recovery would not be an easy one. The doctors weren't sure how much damage his coma had caused. His cognitive skills might have been damaged. His speech, memory, and mobility may have diminished. The doctors didn't know yet. It was too soon to tell.

The only thing that was certain was that his appetite hadn't been affected. He had phoned Rose twice that morning, asking for a breakfast stop at McDonalds, Hardees, and Wendy's. He was like a child who had been weaned from candy, and suddenly, he was allowed to eat whatever candy he wanted.

On previous occasions when Booger's stomach was more influential than his brain, Rose had corralled his food demands. But not this day, not the day after he awakened from the coma. On this day, her husband was going to get any and everything he wanted. She would spoil him today, maybe even for a few days.

By 8:30 am, Rose had made the three fast food stops and had arrived on the third floor of Cox North Hospital. As she arrived at the nurse's station, Nurse Moffitt stopped her. The young, petite woman with baby blue eyes and long brown hair couldn't help but chuckle when she saw Rose carrying several bags of fast food down the hall.

"Bringing food to your husband, Mrs. McClain?" she said with a smile.

"Yes, Diane. He called me twice this morning to put in his requests."

"My goodness, how much food did he ask for?" the nurse remarked, looking at three bags of food and two cups of coffee.

"A lot," Rose said, smiling back. "I had to make three restaurant stops.

"Well, I probably shouldn't tell you, but he's already had two breakfasts from downstairs."

"Oh my. I guess Booger is making up for time."

"Do you need help carrying it to the room?"

"No, I'm fine, Diane."

The two women smiled, and Rose walked down the hallway, around the corner to room 323.

Her husband was sitting up in bed reading a newspaper with an unlit stogie hanging out of his mouth.

"What's that in your mouth, old man?"

"A stogie. I had one of the candy stripers go downstairs and pick me up one."

"You know that you can't smoke in here?"

"Yeah, that's why it's not lit."

"What's the purpose if you can't smoke it?"

"I like the smell. Besides, I might just sneak outside and light it up."

"Over my dead body."

"That can be arranged."

"Then who would bring you all this great fast food?"

"Good point. I'll wait until you're gone to go outside and smoke it."

Rose set the bags of breakfast sandwiches, burritos, and

fried potatoes and the two cups of black coffee down on the bed tray and watched as her husband engulfed an entire sausage, egg, and cheese McMuffin in two large bites and washed it down with steaming hot coffee.

"You know Nurse Diane told me that you've already had two breakfasts from the cafeteria downstairs this morning."

"Snitch."

"Aren't you overdoing it a little?"

"Naugh, just making up for lost time," Booger said as he stuffed a breakfast burrito into his mouth.

Rose smiled and gently rubbed the top of her husband's head with the palm of her hand.

"What's the matter, Rose? Do I have something in my hair?"

"No, old man. I just missed you."

"I missed you, too."

"Booger, I don't know what I would have done if I'd lost you."

"Probably hooked up with some younger, wealthy guy."

"Don't joke about that, Booger. I was serious."

"Don't you know by now, Rose? I'm too tough to die."

"Well, the three bullet holes and the five-minute flat line on the heart monitor might have a different opinion."

"Seriously, Booger, when you're well enough to come home, can we just slow down and take some alone time together? Maybe a long vacation, a second honeymoon?"

"But we didn't take a first one."

"Exactly my point. Every time we plan to get away, a case comes up."

"Let's just go before work interferes with whatever plans we make."

"OK. Where do you want to go?"

"Anyplace. It doesn't matter. Just someplace that's quiet and away from everything, someplace where it's just you and me."

"Maybe a cabin in the woods next to a lake stocked with plenty of catfish."

"The cabin in the woods part I like."

Rose reached for her husband's hand and, with a serious look, said, "Booger, what was it like being in a coma. Did you feel anything? Did you dream?"

"I felt hungry, and I thought about eating a Big Mac," Booger said, reaching for a bacon, egg, and cheese croissant.

"I'm serious, McClain. Did you know I was beside you? Did you hear me talking to you?"

"Do you really want to know?"

"Yes."

"Promise not to think I'm crazy."

"I already think that."

"I was above the clouds in a school room like the one I went to for grade school and with my first-grade teacher."

"OK. Heaven?"

"No."

"Hell?"

"No."

"Purgatory?"

"No. Well, sort of. It was like a waiting room for Heaven. Although they didn't call it Heaven. They called it the City."

"OK. And why were you in a schoolroom with your first-grade teacher?"

"I was supposed to learn about my life so I could make a decision whether to stay or go back home."

"And you decided to come back to me?"

"Yes."

"Oh, sweetie. I'm glad you decided to come back."

"Look, it's hard to explain because my memory is fuzzy. It's like a dream that is fading now, but I don't think it was an easy decision to come back."

"What? Why?"

"Because to come back home, I had to give up the opportunity to go on.. My family, everyone that I loved except for you, was waiting for me there.. It may have been my only opportunity to get to Heaven. In coming back, I might be missing everything."

"And you gave it all up to come back to me?"

"Yes, Rose."

"Why?"

"Because I love you. I couldn't let our life together end, not yet, not that way. You needed me, and when you love someone, you show up for them."

"Ah, sweetie. I'm glad you chose me."

"Me too, Rose."

Rose thought for a few moments before asking, "So, was it a dream? You said it was like a dream."

"No. I believe it was real."

"Did you meet God?"

"No. But I saw Jesus, and I saw the Kangaroo man."

"The Kangaroo man?" Rose asked with a puzzled look. "Okay, so, yeah, it sounds like a dream."

"No. Well, it does sound like that, but it wasn't. It was more real than here. Life is like a dream." "Of course it is, honey," Rose said politely.

Booger could tell his wife was being polite now. "His

name is Samuel. The kangaroo man. He's the one who brought me back to you."

Intrigued, Rose humored her husband. "Oh, like an Angel?"

"No, a fallen angel. Samuel was once an angel, but he made some bad choices, and he was expelled from the City."

"OK. So, he was sent to Hell?" Rose asked with a skeptical voice and a confused look.

"No, there is no Hell, at least in the sense that we think of it. It's not down below and not full of fire and demons. Hell is right here on Earth. It's in hate and prejudice, greed, and temptation. It's in the crimes and sins we do. It's in our lust and betrayal, our lying, and our cheating. Man creates his own Hell by the poor decisions he makes with his own free will."

"Old man, this is getting a little deep for me. Are you sure that coma didn't mess with your brain a little bit?"

"Rose, sweetie, I'm seeing things more clearly than I ever did before."

"OK. Booger?"

"Yes."

"You said the Kangaroo man brought you back to me."

"Yes, that's right."

Rose looked around the room. "Booger, is he still here?"

"No, I suppose not."

"Well, if you see him again in your dreams, thank him for me."

CHAPTER THREE
NURSE DIANE

Diane Moffitt, the young day nurse on the third floor of Cox Hospital, had become good friends with Rose in a short period of time. The attractive woman of twenty-three reminded Rose of a cross between her sister Hope and the daughter Rose always wanted but never had.

The nurse was a shoulder to cry on during some of the most difficult periods of her husband's coma. After her shift was over, Nurse Diane would often sit with Rose in Booger's hospital room, and they would talk. She was a welcome distraction for Rose and helped fill the loneliness for Diane.

The nurse had lost her husband, and it was a loss she had still not gotten over. They had met at the orphanage where both of them lived for much of their lives. John was just twelve days older than Diane, at least according to the birth certificate provided by the State. John never knew for sure if that date was accurate. He had been abandoned on the front steps of a Baptist Church just a few days after his birth.

Both were quiet introverts, really, who kept to themselves and were slow to make friends. They bonded over their mutual interest in playing solitaire and watching old, black and white movies. Their friendship grew over the years as they watched other orphans be adopted while they were left behind.

At the age of eighteen, both were released from the

orphanage to make their way in the world. John was released just two months ahead of Diane, so he tried to scrape together some money before she was released, but he didn't have much luck. Abandoned by the only family they had known and left without a home, they lived on the streets for several weeks until Diane found a job waiting tables at a greasy spoon diner.

A week later, both moved into a subsidized apartment in a rough part of town. A few months later, John joined the Army, and life began to look up for them.

Not long after, they got married and moved to housing just outside of Fort Campbell, where John was stationed.

That was when Diane went to school to become a nurse. The couple was extremely happy together, and both dreamed of building a family.

Diane was five weeks pregnant when her husband was sent to Afghanistan. The war was winding down over there, and both were optimistic that he would not be stationed there for long. Three weeks after he arrived, a roadside bomb claimed her husband's life. The same day Diane got the news about John, she had a miscarriage and lost their baby.

For the most part, Diane hid her loneliness and bouts with depression. After completing nursing school, she moved back to Springfield and took a job at Cox Hospital. A year later, she met Rose while working on the same floor that Booger was on.

With Rose, she had a friend and mother figure who was going through a difficult time. Rose, too, was lonely and in need of companionship. They bonded over their misfortunes.

The relationship between Diane and Rose had changed somewhat since Booger came out of his coma. Their lives were headed in totally different directions. Rose was happy and looking forward to her future with her husband. But Diane found little to look forward to. Time was passing her by, and the friendship she had built with Rose was in jeopardy of fading. Diane had lost her family, her husband, and their child. And now that Booger was back, she sensed that she was in jeopardy of losing the only friend she had. What she didn't understand was that Rose had few good friends over her lifetime, and she had no intention of abandoning Diane.

Rose knew little about her new girlfriend's difficult past. Diane had shielded her from much that had happened in her life. They were skeletons in her closet that she had no intention of letting out.

Before becoming an orphan, life for Diane had been happy and relatively normal until the age of five. Her father's family was well off. They owned several properties in the Springfield market, including a large theatre that was one of the first theatres in the country to show talking films. Diane's great-grandfather had made a small fortune in the stock market in the early '20s and had invested that money into property scattered throughout Springfield.

Her father did not follow in the family business but had been successful in his own right selling commercial plastics. He made a good living, enough to purchase a large home and support a family of five. His wife stayed home with her three children, of which Diane was the oldest. Her brother Nathan was three, and her baby sister Anna had just turned one.

Bob, her father, traveled a lot and was usually gone for weeks at a time. But, when he was at home, he was a good father, spending time with his children and being attentive to Diane's mother, Georgia.

Life was good for the Lander's family during those early years. But, beneath the surface of their idyllic lives was darkness that would shatter her world.

In May of 2006, Sophia Landers, the matriarch of the Landers family, was killed in an automobile accident. D.J., her husband of 47 years, was devastated. He isolated himself from friends and backed away from the day-to-day activities of the family business.

Most people familiar with the Landers businesses assumed Cornilus Landers, the eldest son of Sophia and D.J., would take control. He was the Vice President of the corporation and had been second in command behind D. J.

But Cornilus was not well-liked within the organization. He was weak as a leader and had made numerous bad business decisions. So much so that his father had taken most of his business responsibilities away from him, making his position within the company ostensible.

It was during those few months after the death of Mrs. Landers that the fight for control of Landers Theatre, along with other properties owned by D.J. and Sophia, became intense. Two sons, Cornilus and Brandon, and a daughter, Ida, all working in the family business, fought for more control of the family fortune.

Sophia Landers had been the glue that held the family together. Now, it was greed that was trying to tear it apart.

D.J., numbed with grief, watched as his children tore the family apart, all for power and fortune.

Bob Landers was the exception. Long ago, he chose to walk away from the family business and create his own path in life. The death of his mother and the incapacity of his father to run the business did not change that. And thus, he avoided the intense fighting that took place between his other siblings.

A few months after his wife passed away, D.J.'s grief got the best of him. He chose to hang himself from the third-floor balcony of his spacious home.

The funeral was spectacular. The grieving, for the most part, was counterfeit. D.J. had made many more enemies than he had friends during his lifetime. He was a difficult man, driven more by greed than by empathy. It was a family trait that most of the Landers family had inherited.

The pretense of mourning lasted right up to the reading of the will.

As the Landers' siblings gathered in anticipation of a sudden windfall, the family attorney had news that none of them anticipated. D.J. had written a new will just days before his death. And the details of that revised will would prove devastating for some of the Landers' children.

The estate and all stock would be sold and divided equally between all four of the Landers' children. All the businesses except one would be divided equally by Cornilus, Brandon, and Ida.

Each would own one-third of each business.

The only business not handed over to the three siblings was the Landers Theatre. That business was given to Bob Landers.

Bob, the only child of Sophia and D.J. who hadn't gone into the family business, who hadn't fought to gain control of the family fortune, now found himself the owner of the most profitable entity within the family business.

As the other siblings would soon find out, D.J. Landers had not been the successful businessman that he had portrayed. His company was nearly bankrupt.

After his death, much of the Landers' estate would be sold to pay off creditors. Many of the businesses the family owned had lost money for years. Everything the three siblings inherited that day was nearly worthless.

The only property that had made money was the Landers Theatre, and now that was owned by Bob Landers. To say that the other Landers' siblings were upset with the consequences of that will would be an understatement.

Bob Landers, the only child of D.J. and Sophia, who had absolutely no interest in being in the family business, was suddenly the sole owner of the most profitable entity of his father's estate.

D.J. Landers had paid his children back for their selfishness and greed. He knew that his empire was about to crumble, and had separated his only profitable business from the others and had given it to the only son who had not been afflicted with greed, hatred, and betrayal.

A few months into his newfound fortune, Bob, Georgia, and their kids had planned to attend a family Christmas party hosted by Ida Landers. It was an attempt to reconcile the siblings and their families, three days before Christmas.

Diane was the only child who would not accompany her parents to that Christmas party. The day before, she came down with the flu, and Sophia scrambled to find a babysitter to watch her while Nathan and Anna went with their parents.

It was cold on December 22nd, but the skies were clear, and there was no snow or ice on the roads.

The police who arrived at the scene of the accident could not find a reason why the car went out of control and veered off the highway. It was an unexplainable, tragic accident. Maybe the driver fell asleep. Perhaps they were distracted, or maybe another car came into their lane, forcing them off the road. There were no witnesses, at least no witnesses that came forward.

Bob, Georgia, Nathan, and Anna Landers were all killed early that evening.

Diane would become an orphan overnight. Georgia had no living relatives. Bob had two brothers and a sister. But not one of the three stepped forward to take Diane in. She was sent to a Catholic orphanage in Nixa, MO. There, she would spend the next dozen years of her life. They weren't easy years.

Assets owned by her parents were sold and put into a trust account that would be hers on her 21st birthday. The Landers Theatre was included in those assets. Although management and operational control were given to her uncles and aunt, until the trust account became hers.

On her 21st birthday, the widow who had known so much tragedy and grief in life suddenly became wealthy.

Unlike his father, Bob Landers was a very successful businessman. He had left an estate worth millions to his only surviving daughter.

And even with all that money, Diane Landers Moffitt continued to live a simple life. She remained unspoiled from her sudden riches, and few people had any idea how wealthy she was.

CHAPTER FOUR
THE FRIENDSHIP BETWEEN ROSE AND DIANE

Diane had no real friends. The children she knew in the orphanage came and went so often that Diane became afraid to get too close to anyone because once she did, they left, and she was alone again. Her life was a lonely existence in those days. The only lasting friendship Diane had was with John Carver.

John Carver was not his birth name. No one knew what it was. Sister Agnes gave that name to him. Over the years at the orphanage, the bond and friendship between him and Diane grew. They were almost inseparable.

The three-story orphanage run by the Sisters of St. Mary's was over 80 years old, and the building showed the wear and tear of age.

Rooms were cold in the winter and hot in the summer. The old furnace in the basement was on its last leg and could barely warm the first floor. It creaked and moaned when it started up and smelled like gas every time the blowers kicked in.

A few of the nuns were cruel. Some were sadistic. The worst was Sister Agnes. She was in her mid-fifties, going on seventy-five. She looked old, way beyond her years. Short, thinning gray hair, dark eyes, thick wrinkles on a weather-worn face, and carried a wart the size of a golf ball on her right cheek. The edge of her lips arched downward, a sign of a miserable life and a face that rarely smiled.

Sister Agnes took a particular interest in Diane. The nun loved dispensing discipline and seemed to be on a mission to make Diane's life as hellish as possible. Sister Agnes carried a metal ruler with her wherever she went and loved using it to slap children on the wrists any chance she could. If someone got out of line in the lunch hall, slap! If someone took too long in the bathroom, slap! John once got slapped for sneezing in class. Sister Agnes' eyes glinted with glee every time she got to use her favorite weapon. But the worst punishment was the basement. Any sign of open disobedience, such as talking back or taking too long in the bathroom, would result in a night in the basement.

The basement of Sisters of St. Mary's Orphanage was haunted. The children all knew it to be so and dreaded the threat of having to spend a night down there. Diane spent weeks at a time inside its cinder block walls and six-foot ceiling.

The basement was cold, damp, and dark, with only one 60-watt ceiling bulb providing any light. There were no windows. If it rained, water would seep in through gaps in the cinder block walls. Bugs, spiders, and rats would seek refuge in the rain. An occasional snake would slither in. Hungry rats were the worst. Three small meals a day would be brought down those creaky, wooden basement stairs. That was when the rats gathered to feast on any morsels that fell.

At bedtime, the ceiling light would be turned off, and the nightmares would begin. The old furnace would provide the only light when it turned on to provide heat to the floors above. It was loud and made eerie noises that made it difficult for Diane to sleep.

On cold nights, the rats would curl up next to Diane to feed off the warmth of her body.

It was during those dark, cold nights that the ghosts

would appear in the glow of that old coal furnace. There were weird sounds and strange shadows. At first, Diane thought it was figments of her imagination, ghostly figures that came out in nightmares and disappeared when she opened her eyes. So, she closed her eyes tightly and counted to ten. Then, she opened them.

A frightening figure, head three sizes too big with warts covering its face and horns protruding out of its head, was lying next to her and looking straight into her eyes.

Diane tried to scream, but nothing came out of her mouth. Her voice was frozen from fright.

Sleeping at night after that was nearly impossible during her stays in the basement. And there were many more ghosts and dark shadowy figures that were illuminated in the light of that furnace, too many to count.

Diane never knew it, but Sister Agnes had a financial reason to treat her cruelly. The building and land that St. Mary's Orphanage occupied were owned by the Landers children. Cornilus, the oldest and most evil of the children, had threatened to close the orphanage if the Sisters could not find a way to break Diane Landers' spirit. As a result, the other Sisters closed their eyes to the cruelty that Sister Agnes inflicted on Diane.

They tried to drive her crazy and certainly came close to doing so. She was passed up for every adoption, was isolated from the other children, ignored and unloved by the Sisters, and spent the majority of her time alone in that basement.

Through all of her ordeals, John was there to make her life a little more bearable. He paid the price for his friendship with Diane. He was passed over for every adoption and would spend all his pre-adult years in that orphanage as a result.

If their goal was to drive Diane crazy, to make it impossible for her to inherit and run the Landers Theatre when she turned twenty-one, the Landers children did not succeed.

The daughter of Bob and Georgia Landers was every bit as strong-willed as her parents. She left the orphanage on her 18th birthday and never looked back.

John and Diane moved in together. Diane took a graveyard shift at a greasy-spoon diner, then got a late-night shift at the local 3M plant. When John enlisted, they married, moved to Fort Campbell, and she attended nursing school.

The Landers' girl was driven, even obsessed with making something of herself. It wasn't that money motivated her because it didn't. And it wasn't that she cared about status because that didn't motivate her either. She just wanted to be happy and to forget those miserable years at St. Mary's Orphanage.

It wasn't surprising that her friendship with Rose grew during the period Booger was in a coma. After all, Diane was a good, caring, empathetic person. She had her share of heartaches in her life and could relate to what Rose was going through.

But the thing that drew her to Rose more than anything was her need for friendship. Diane hadn't had a friend for a very long time. Rose made her smile and laugh. She couldn't even remember the last time she had laughed.

Even as Booger came out of his coma and he became stronger, Rose and Diane's friendship continued to grow. They spent hours together after Diane's shift was over, in Booger's room, right up to the time visiting hours were over.

Booger found it difficult to get a word in with both of them talking nearly non-stop. He referred to the two of them as Cheech and Chong.

"That just doesn't make any sense," Rose told him after the first time he called them that.

"Sure, it does," Booger responded. "Just like Cheech and Chong, you two ramble to the point it doesn't make any sense to anyone who's sober."

"So, I suppose, if you were three sheets to the wind, our conversations would make sense to you?"

"No, but I wouldn't mind listening to them as much."

"Men," Rose quipped back.

"Yeah, men," Diane agreed.

If truth be told, Booger liked having Diane around. She was a good friend to Rose, and since Hope had died, his wife needed a good friend. Besides, Diane encouraged Rose to provide her husband the simple pleasures he craved: fast food, his stogies, and an occasional glass of rye whiskey. Rose brought him his sausage, egg, and cheese McMuffins for breakfast along with that day's newspaper and fresh black coffee, Double cheese, and fries for lunch, and pizza for dinner. She brought him a fresh stogie every day. He couldn't smoke it, but he liked to hold it in his mouth and smell the tobacco. The rye whiskey she occasionally snuck in her purse at night and poured him a stiff drink just before bedtime, being careful to put the bottle back in her purse before leaving.

Rose babied her husband, and Diane encouraged her.

"Diane, do you have a boyfriend?" Rose asked one day.

"No."

"Why not?" Rose asked. "You'd make a great wife."

"I just haven't met the right man yet, I guess."

"We'll have to do something about that," Rose added with a smile while winking at her husband.

Booger rolled his eyes.

A few minutes later, the doctor entered the room. Unlike his normal stoic self, Dr. Bloomberg was smiling.

"OK, doc. You're freaking me out with that smile. What's going on?" Booger asked.

"You're going home tomorrow, Mr. McClain."

"That's great news," Rose chimed in, giving her husband a big kiss.

"Why, doc? Did my insurance company refuse to pay you anymore?"

"Maybe. That wouldn't surprise me, but no, we're releasing you because you're strong as a bear, and quite frankly, the nurses are getting sick of you."

Diane smiled and nodded in agreement.

"Well, I think that calls for a celebration," Rose said, winking at Diane.

"Great," Booger said, ignoring the wink to Diane. "I'll take a last meal of Filet Mignon, loaded baked potato, and cherry pie à la mode. Then I'll top it off with a stogie and bottle of rye whiskey."

"I'm afraid not, Mr. McClain," the doctor said. "It seems that despite you eating hospital food for the last month, you've managed to gain 10 pounds. You may be my first patient to actually gain weight on a hospital food diet."

Rose snickered.

After the doctor left, Rose turned to her husband with a stern look. "You know, Booger, I'm going to need to put you on a strict diet when you come home until you lose that extra weight."

"Augh, Rose."

"Don't augh at me, old man. It's all that fast food you've had me bring you. I've felt sorry for you until now, but not anymore. When you come home, we're going to walk every evening, and you're going on a diet full of greens and lean meats."

Then Rose's attention turned to Diane. "What do you

say you follow me back to our house, and we can sit at the bar in Booger's man cave and finish off a bottle or two of his rye whiskey and maybe even smoke a stogie."

"Don't you dare, Rose Marie."

"Don't think there is anything you can do about it, old man, at least not tonight, sitting here in your hospital bed."

Later that night, after visiting hours, Diane followed Rose back to her house. It was the first time Diane had been there.

"This place is incredible," Diane said in amazement as Rose gave her a complete tour of the building.

"It's an old warehouse," Rose said with a smile. "Booger built it before we were married. I helped design the house. But it's been rebuilt three times since then."

"The house or the office?" Diane asked.

"Both."

"Why?"

"It's a long story, but let me just say that my husband has made a few enemies over the years."

"Oh, he seems like such a nice guy."

"He's a teddy bear," Rose said with a smile. "A teddy bear with a knack for finding trouble."

"I guess being a detective can be dangerous work."

"Yes."

"Is it because of that work that you have so many surveillance cameras? My, there must be about twenty of them."

"Twenty-eight at last count. I can't be sure. My husband adds them all the time, and sometimes he doesn't tell me about it."

"Why so many?"

"Like I said, he has a knack for finding trouble, and he likes to know who's coming to visit. Each camera has a purpose, and together, they give us a view of every part of the building, inside and out."

"Even inside your house?"

Rose laughed. "No, that's where I put my foot down. There are no video cameras inside our home. But outside the house, every part is covered. No one can come to our door or enter our yard without us seeing them."

"That must make you as safe as possible."

"Yeah, for the most part. But, like I said, we've had our share of trouble. The fact is that if someone is determined to get inside, there is always a way. That's why we have both a safe room on the third floor and a way to escape if need be."

After touring the offices, Rose led her friend down the hallway on the first floor to a large open area that led to her home. That open area was the only part of the building that looked like a warehouse. Concrete floor, brick walls, twelve-foot ceiling, and large windows.

"The large glass windows are bullet-proof, and they're like the one-way glass you see in police interrogation rooms. We can see out, but no one on the outside can see in."

"My, this place is like a fortress."

"Yes, that's the way Booger wants it."

In the far-right corner of the warehouse, Rose pulled out a brick just a couple of inches, and a door opened up on the right side. "You can't even tell there is a door there," Rose said. "It's completely hidden and only opens up when a particular brick is pulled out."

Inside were all the trappings of a normal house. From the entrance, the kitchen and dining area were to the right, and to the left, down a hallway, was the master bedroom, as well as a bathroom and a door that opened to a large man cave. "I designed most of the house, except for the man cave. I let him design it."

Inside the man cave was a large, dark, cherry wood bar area with six barstools. Behind the bar were shelves full of unopened rye whiskey bottles with whiskey glasses hanging above the bar. To the right was a movie theatre with eight oversized leather reclining chairs and a 120-inch wall-mounted screen, and in the back was a separate room with a lock that scanned fingerprints to unlock. Inside were a dozen television monitors, each one feeding into three to four surveillance cameras covering just about every inch of the building and parking lot.

"My goodness," Diane said. "Does someone monitor these cameras?"

"No need to," Rose answered.

"Each surveillance feed has its own motion detector. If anything moves within sight of any of the cameras, an alarm goes off on our cellphones, and we're alerted. Most of the time, it's nothing more than an animal crossing the parking lot, one of us setting the motion detector off, or the mailman with a package delivery. A quick scan of the monitors will tell us if we should be concerned. The third floor of the office has an identical room, so if we're working, we can easily check the monitors."

"How do you know which one to check?"

"See the light above each monitor?"

"Yes."

"It will light up red if that is the monitor that shows motion."

"Wow. That's incredible."

After the tour, Rose invited Diane to sit down at the bar and have a drink.

"What do you have, Rose?"

"Well, Diane, we just don't have many visitors here. I'm

afraid the liquor assortment is pretty small. Booger is really the only one that drinks here, and, as you can see, he is a fan of rye whiskey, and except for an occasional beer, that's all he drinks."

"Well, I'll have a beer then. What do you have?"

Rose opened the refrigerator to show about three dozen cans of Pabst Blue Ribbon Tall Boys. "All we have is Pabst. That's the only beer Booger drinks."

"Do they still make it?"

"Yeah, but it's hard to find. Booger buys from a liquor store in town that special orders ten cases at a time for him."

"I think I'll pass. Anything else?"

"In the back of the refrigerator is a box of white wine."

"In a box?"

"Yeah."

"What kind of white wine?"

"I don't know. The box just says, 'white wine.'"

"It may have been in here a while, too. It's giving off a strange smell."

"I think I'll take a rye whiskey with water on the rocks."

"Good choice. I'll have the same."

Rose grabbed two short glasses from above the bar, poured a shot of whiskey in them, three ice cubes, and filled the remainder with water. They toasted to their friendship and the recovery of Booger, and then both women took a sip of the concoction. Both, almost in unison, began coughing.

"Damn, that's strong," Diane said, curling her lips.

Neither woman drank alcohol very often, and especially not liquor. The drinks were weak but not weak enough for them. For nearly two hours, they laughed and cried and talked nonstop.

Diane talked about her childhood and the death of her parents and siblings. She talked about the orphanage and confided in Rose about the large inheritance she received on her twenty-first birthday. And she talked about the Landers Theatre.

As the night grew later, the drinks grew stronger. What began as a shot of alcohol in the glasses became two or three shots. Less water, less ice, and much more alcohol.

Both were slurring their speech. Each was laughing for no apparent reason. Their friendship was growing, and their inhibitions were slipping away.

"I've got to tell you something, Rose."

"What? Girlfriend, you can tell me anything."

"Cornilus Landers is greedy. All he cares about is money, and he hates me because I've got it, and he doesn't. I think he's been stealing from the Landers Theatre. I'm not an accountant, but I've looked at the books, and things just don't add up."

"Are you sure?"

"Not absolutely positive, but I think so. And Brandon and Ida may be involved, too. The theater has been packed almost every performance, but according to the books, it's losing money. It just doesn't make any sense."

"Maybe you should hire a professional to examine the books."

"I have. I've asked a local CPA firm to come in next week and go over everything."

"Do the Landers kids know about it?"

"I haven't told them, but I have a suspicion that they have an idea that something's up. Yesterday, I received a call from Cornilus Landers asking me to meet him and his siblings tomorrow night at Landers after the performance."

Rose put her hand on Diane's shoulder. "Do you want me to go to the meeting?"

"Oh, no. I appreciate the offer, but I think it's something I need to do alone."

"Did Cornilus tell you what the meeting was about?"

"Just business," he said.

Rose showed a concerned look. "I don't think you should go there alone, late at night. Couldn't you ask them to schedule a meeting during the day?"

"Cornilus said that late in the evening was the only time all three of them could get together. Besides, it's not easy for me to get off work, so it works better for me too."

"Please, Diane, be careful."

CHAPTER FIVE
BOOGER GOES HOME

Rose's head was pounding the next morning when her alarm went off at 5 am. She rolled over and hit the snooze button, and ten minutes later did it again, and again, ten minutes after.

Finally, she sat up and slowly walked to the bathroom. After a hot shower and three cups of strong black coffee, she was ready to go to see her husband.

A stop at McDonalds and the newspaper stand, and twenty minutes later, she walked into his room, expecting to see him dressed and ready to come home. But there he was, sitting up in bed, reading a newspaper with an unsmoked stogie hanging out of his mouth.

"Where have you been, Rose?"

"Booger, it's only 7am."

"Yeah, well, I figured you'd be here an hour ago. I had to send Nurse Diane downstairs to get me a newspaper, coffee, and a cinnamon roll."

"Booger, you knew that I'd bring you breakfast. Couldn't you wait? Besides, I assume the hospital is sending up a breakfast for you."

"Already come and gone. The cinnamon roll was dessert."

"And the food I've brought you?"

"The second course."

"Geez, sweetie. No wonder you've gained weight. So,

have you seen the doctor?"

"No, he's probably still sleeping?"

"Any word on when you'll be able to go home?"

"Well, yes and no."

"What?"

"Yes, I know when I can go home, but I don't know what time that's going to be."

"Booger, my head is pounding. What in the world do you mean?"

"The night nurse came in about 4 am and checked my blood pressure and temperature. Then she put some odd contraption on my index finger."

"That would be to measure your oxygen level."

"OK. Well, I must not have passed because a few minutes later, another nurse came in and did it again."

"And?"

"And then she brought in this breathing tube with a ball at the bottom," Booger said, holding the device up. She said I need to breathe into it every fifteen minutes and that the ball needs to go above this line."

"So, what was your oxygen level?"

"87."

"What's it supposed to be?"

"90 or higher. She said the doctor won't release me until it reads 90 or higher."

"Well, what are you supposed to do?"

"Breath into this contraption every fifteen minutes and walk down the hall every thirty minutes until it goes above 90."

Everyone wanted Booger to go home that day – the detective himself, Rose, Diane, the nurses, his doctor, and even the cafeteria people who prepared and delivered his food. The only exception might be the area's fast food restaurants that had seen an uptick in business since he came out of his coma.

So, it became a group effort to get his oxygen level above 90. Nurses took turns watching him breathe into the oxygen monitor. Then walked with him down the hall and back, checking his oxygen level afterwards. The first several trips were not successful. But the final trip down the hall at 1:00 pm resulted in an oxygen level of 90 for three brief seconds before falling below.

The doctor, anxious to get rid of one of his most challenging patients, signed off on his release, pretending to ignore the fact that it had dipped below 90 again.

Booger McClain was home an hour later.

There, he would become Rose's most challenging patient.

"Bring me my stogie, sweetie; I want a glass of Rye Whiskey, tall, no water, one ice cube, and put the cube in first so it doesn't dilute the flavor of the whiskey; I'm hungry. Can you make a run to McDonalds? Get me another blanket and turn up the volume on the television."

"Buford McClain," Rose shouted in a mostly controlled but slightly upset voice. "You know darn well that the doctor said no alcohol and no tobacco for two days or until your oxygen level was in the mid-90s. Plus, you're supposed to breathe into that device every fifteen minutes and keep the ball above the line for ten seconds each time."

"Rose, I feel fine, and I think, considering all that I've been through, I deserve a couple of life's little luxuries. Is that too much to ask?" Booger said in a quiet, sad voice, trying without success to produce a single teardrop.

"I'm not buying it, old man. Going without your precious cigars and whiskey for a couple of days is a small sacrifice for your well-being."

"For you, it's a small sacrifice. For me, it's practically inhumane."

"Too bad. I've already put a lock on the whiskey cabinet and on the drawer that holds your stogies. I'll remove the locks in two days, provided your oxygen level is back to normal."

"OK, Nurse Ratched."

"Oh, that's funny because you know that you're the one driving me to the cuckoo's nest."

That night, Rose made her husband one of his favorite dinners, ribeye steak, medium rare, topped with grilled mushrooms and onions, American fries with onions and red peppers, buttermilk biscuits with butter and strawberry jam, and cherry pie warm from the oven and topped with plenty of vanilla ice cream. It wasn't healthy, but she was so glad to have her man home that she told him – after some begging – that he could have one last good meal in his home before she got strict again. Not too long ago, she, herself, had begged God for such an opportunity.

The table was set with a white tablecloth and two candles, as well as a glass of wine for her and a cup of coffee for him.

Booger, looking over the feast in front of him, turned to Rose with a smile and said, "Sweetie, are you trying to seduce me?"

"Old man, the only thing your eyes are hungry for is the food in front of you."

"Maybe, but you're looking awfully good for dessert."

"Better than the cherry pie and ice cream I made for you?"

"Well, that's a tough choice."

They joked and laughed and held hands as if it were their very first date. And, in a way, it may have seemed like it was. Booger had come back from the dead. He and Rose had a second chance. Neither doubted that they would ever take their love for granted again. And both thanked God that they had a little more time together.

That night, they cuddled in bed, talked, and joked with each other until well after midnight. They had always loved each other, but the possibility of losing each other had drawn them even closer together.

They fell asleep that night, cuddling and holding hands just like they did on their wedding night.

For a brief moment, it seemed all was right in the world.

CHAPTER SIX
THE MAN ON THE STAIRS

The sun penetrated through the curtains just before 7 am, and it was enough to wake Booger McClain up from a restless sleep, sweating profusely and breathing heavily. His dreams, so normal early in his sleep, had quickly been haunted by a dark shadow figure that had been chasing him up and down Walnut Street. Suddenly, the dream switched to much more of a nightmare. The kangaroo man appeared on old wooden stairs, smiling, then laughing, but not a normal laugh, an almost sadistic laugh. He was pointing down to a dark, dungeon-like basement where a body lay on the floor. Booger couldn't make the figure on the floor out at first. Then, his vision focused on a woman. She lay on her stomach, alive but dazed, moaning in pain, a young woman. Slowly, she began to roll on her side, and when she did, Booger recognized her. The woman was Diane Landers.

For several minutes, Booger sat on the side of the bed, looking outside through a small opening in the curtains, waiting for his heart rate to slow and the sweat to stop dripping down his cheeks. When he had settled, Booger turned in the bed to see that Rose was not in the bed with him. Then he glanced at the clock. Almost 8 am. *Rose had probably been up for at least two hours by now,* he thought. She had let him sleep in.

So, Booger showered, shaved, and changed clothes. Then he decided it was time to join her in the kitchen. He could smell the strong, black Folgers' coffee that his wife had brewing, and with every step, his pace quickened. Suddenly, he stopped dead in his tracks. His nose had detected the undeniable aroma of bacon frying in the Rose's old cast-iron skillet.

"Could it be? Could it really be?"

"It be," Rose said with a quick smile before returning her attention to the stovetop, where she had eggs and gravy cooking too.

"B-b-b-bacon!" Booger could barely spit the words out.

Rose had been serving her husband a variety of spinach and kale-based Danishes for breakfast for years to keep his high blood pressure in check, but she figured he needed something heartier since he was in recovery.

An oven timer dinged before she could respond. "And biscuits, too. I'm pulling those out now."

"I thought maybe I'd died again," Booger said.

"No, I gotta build you back up before I kill you with the healthy stuff," she said, grinning.

"Well, honey, you know best," he said as he wafted the smells dramatically towards his nose.

After a moment of suspended bliss created by savory sensory overload, Booger was brought back down to Earth when he remembered the nightmare he had about his wife's new friend.

"Any word from Diane yet?"

"No."

After stuffing three strips of bacon in his mouth and wolfing down a gravy-soaked butternut biscuit, he gave his stomach a short break and lifted his head to smile at his wife.

"OK, I know that look, Booger. What's on your mind?"

"Rose, remember how much fun we had exploring the haunted streets of downtown Hannibal?"

"I wouldn't exactly call it fun. Some of those places scared the be-Jesus out of me."

"Yeah, but then you'd beg me to hold you tight."

"OK, so you had fun torturing me?"

"No, sweetie. Both of us had fun. I remember?"

"Is this your way of saying that you're losing your memory? Is this the early stages of Alzheimer's?"

"Babe, what I'm trying to say is that I think we should take a little vacation, just the two of us, to recharge our batteries, so to speak."

Rose perked up and smiled from cheek to cheek. "Honey, you're reading my mind, and I know the perfect place to go, Key West."

"No, Rose."

"Hawaii?"

"Afraid not."

"Europe?"

"I was thinking a little closer to home."

"Arkansas? Alabama? Georgia?"

"No, honey, none of those places has what we have practically in our backyard."

"Oh, I hate to ask, but what's that?"

"Ghosts."

"That, I would have never guessed."

"Rose, what do you say, the two of us take a closer examination of some of Springfield's most haunted locations?"

"I would say, no! You know I like the idea of a good haunted hotel, but I'd prefer something that wasn't in our backyard."

"Come on, Rose. We can go to Pythian Castle, the Vandivort Theatre, and even the Walnut Inn."

"No, especially not the Walnut Inn. I actually think that

place really is haunted."

"And we obviously have to go to The Landers Theatre."

"You've already scheduled this little getaway, haven't you, Buford McClain?"

"Well, yes. I thought it would be fun."

"Do you think going eight blocks down the street to frighten the be-Jesus out of me will be fun?"

"Well, for me, it will be."

Rose shot her husband a nasty look.

"The best thing is, Rose, that this will be like a real vacation. I've booked us for five days and four nights at the incredible Walnut Street Bed and Breakfast. No cooking, no cleaning, just relaxation and fun."

"When?"

"When, what?"

"When did you book the Walnut Street Bed and Breakfast, McClain? You've been with me or asleep ever since you got home."

"OK, Rose. I haven't booked it yet, but I'm getting ready to."

"Well, then. I've got one word for you. 'Don't.'"

"Come on. Just the two of us alone. It will be fun."

"Booger, has anyone told you that your brand of fun leaves a lot to be desired?"

"You have. Several times, I believe."

"OK, Booger. I'll go along with you on this because it will make you happy and because I'm sure you spent quite a bit of time putting this mini-vacation together in your mind."

"About five minutes."

"But Booger, in the future, when planning anything involving the two of us, it might be best to remember that someday I will be the one picking out a nursing home for you."

"Yes, dear."

Booger had an ulterior motive for choosing the hauntings of Springfield for a mini vacation. Yes, it was cheap, and yes, he liked how close Rose held on to him whenever she was scared, but mostly, it was because of Diane Landers and the nightmare he had involving her the night before.

Diane was Rose's best friend, her only friend, and she had not been heard from since attending a late-night meeting at the Landers the night before.

"Did his nightmare mean anything?" Booger wasn't sure. *"Probably not,"* he thought. But the detective in him needed to know.

So, after breakfast, he called the Walnut Street Bed & Breakfast and made reservations for four nights beginning that evening.

Two hours later, they had packed and loaded up the car and were on their way in Booger's Apple red 1969 Corvette convertible. It was a cool afternoon, and the wind was whipping as Rose tightened her scarf and curled up in a blanket in the passenger seat.

"You realize, old man, that it is cold and windy with about an 80 percent chance of rain."

"So, what's your point, sweetie?"

"My point is that it's too freakin' cold and windy to have the top down."

"Darling, the fresh air is good for both of us."

"You know that cowboy hat you're wearing is going to blow right off your head in about ten seconds."

"Nah, my head is perfectly shaped to keep this hat on no matter how windy it gets."

Fifteen seconds later, a strong gust of wind picked up his hat and blew it into the back seat. Out of the corner of his eye, Booger could see Rose smiling.

Thunder and lightning began sounding within the deep, dark clouds.

"Booger, how long does it take you to put the top back up in this car?"

"I don't know. About thirty seconds, I guess."

"Then I suggest you start putting it up now," she said as the first raindrops began to fall.

By the time the top was completely up again, it was pouring rain. No one said a word. Booger glanced out of the corner of his right eye to see his wife completely soaked. The scarf she tightened to keep her hair in place had flown away, and his wife's hair had fallen to a soggy mess. Rose was no longer smiling.

With the top up and Rose in no mood to talk, Booger turned the radio on to 100.5 the Wolf. The first country song that played was "Rain Is a Good Thing" by Luke Bryant. From the corner of his eye, Booger could see a darkening frown spread over his wife's wet face. He immediately turned the dial to 94.7 KTTS, where local news was just beginning.

"Woman's body found at the bottom of the basement stairs at Landers Theatre this morning," the announcer began.

CHAPTER SEVEN
THE DEATH OF DIANE LANDERS

Much like the nightmare Booger had the night before, Diane Landers' lifeless body was found at the bottom of the basement stairs at Landers Theatre. She was discovered by the cleaning crew that came in early the next morning.

Rose was distraught. Her only friend was gone, and although the police were quick to rule her death accidental, Rose felt otherwise.

"Booger, she went there to meet the Landers siblings. Where were they? Why didn't one of them report her death? No, there is something wrong. A late-night meeting: suspicion of money gone missing and possibly the books being tampered with. It just doesn't add up."

Booger took a right turn and headed for the Springfield Police Department. He and Rose needed to get some answers.

Detective Walker Jelks had been with the Springfield Police Department for 33 years. He was a rookie cop the year the Springfield Three disappeared in the middle of the night. Booger first met him during his investigation of the disappearance of the three women.

They weren't exactly friends, but both men respected each other. Walker Jelks had worked his way up from street cop to Detective in less than five years. He was known to be tough but fair and honest. His toughness had resulted in a half dozen harassment and intimidation complaints over the years that had drawn unwanted attention to the SPD, which ultimately limited the detective's advancement opportunities within the department.

Married four times, Jelks had finally found a woman who would tolerate him. Her name was Merna, and they were deeply in love, although Jelks wasn't the type of man to wear his emotions on his sleeves. He blamed his previous marital woes on his dedication to his job and the excessive hours he worked. His ex-wives had a different opinion of the troubles. Detective Jelks had two addictions. His love of cheap whiskey and his lust for cheap women. He spent most of his off-duty hours at Big Curly's Country Bar on the city's northwest side. It was a rundown relic of the 60s that attracted the kind of clientele that the detective often investigated. Jelks liked to joke that when "Friends in Low Places" was written, Garth Brooks was singing about Big Curly's. Merna changed all that in the five short years they had been married. Jelks still had a passion for cheap whiskey, but he had given up the cheap women.

Unable to bear children and diagnosed with cancer two years earlier, Merna had seen better times. Despite, or maybe as a result of their troubles, Jelks and his wife had never been closer. He had even planned to retire at the end of the year and take his wife to Tahiti for a second honeymoon. She had often dreamed of going there and had even hung a picture of a hut at sunrise on the crystal blue waters of Tahiti over their fireplace.

Despite his walks on the dark side, Detective Jelks was an honest cop and had a reputation for digging for the truth. Those were the qualities that Booger respected in him.

"I need to see Detective Jelks," Booger said to the sergeant working at the front desk.

"What's it in regard to?" the sergeant asked.

"The death of Diane Landers," Booger replied. "Tell him that Booger McClain has some information for him."

A couple of minutes later, the sergeant came back, opened the door, and said, "Follow me."

Booger and Rose walked through a large open area where several patrolmen were working into a narrow hallway to another room, smaller in size but with three plain-clothed detectives working at desks. One of them, Booger recognized as belonging to Walker Jelks.

A few feet from his desk, Jelks looked up from the file he was reading and said, "Shit, McClain, what the hell do you want?"

"It's good to see you, too, Jelks," Booger said. "This is my wife, Rose," he added, noticing the detective's stare in Rose's direction.

"OK, McClain and Mrs. McClain, take a seat. Tell me what's so damn important you had to come down here to disturb my wonderful day. But make it quick. I'm busy."

The detective looked like he hadn't been home to shower and change for several days. His shirt was wrinkled with numerous food stains, and his tie was loose and put on crooked. From three feet away, Booger could smell the cheap whisky on the detective's breath.

"It's about the death of Diane Landers," Booger began. "There's some information that I think you should know."

"Let me stop you right there, McClain. Ms. Landers' death has already been ruled accidental. The case is closed, so there's no need for any more information."

"Did you know that Diane Landers had a late-night meeting at the theatre with Cornilus, Brandon, and Ida Landers?"

"Yes, I knew that McClain. We've already got statements from the Landers kids. They had a meeting with Diane Landers at 10 pm last night in the theatre to discuss her role in the management of the theatre. The meeting lasted about an hour. Then, she remained there to take a look at the books and upcoming events. The Landers siblings left."

"No one stayed around to show her where everything was and to lock up?" Rose asked.

"Diane Landers was aware that everything she wanted to look at was in the office, and that was located downstairs in the basement. As for locking up, Ms. Landers had her own set of keys and was quite capable of turning out the lights and locking up when she was through."

"It just doesn't make sense, detective. Diane Landers was concerned about that meeting. I even suggested that I go with her," Rose said. "She suspected that someone was embezzling money from the theatre and had even hired a CPA to examine the books the following day. Knowing that the CPA was going to thoroughly examine the books the next day, why would she stick around to look at them that night? Diane wasn't an accountant. She had no idea what to look for. No, it just doesn't make sense that she would stick around."

"I assure you that it does make sense, Mrs. McClain. More than likely, she wanted to gather all the information that the CPA needed to examine and take it home with her so she could provide it to the CPA the next day, and he could look it all over in his office rather than in the basement of the theatre where he would likely have prying eyes looking over his shoulder."

"So, detective, she decides to stick around by herself in a dark, spooky theatre, then go downstairs into an even spookier basement to look for something that may or may not be there and something that she wasn't even certain exactly what she was looking for," Rose said in a voice that sounded more like an adult talking to a child that was providing a story that just didn't make any sense.

"Yes," the detective replied confidently.

"So, what exactly caused her death, detective?"

"She died of a broken neck sustained in a fall down the basement stairs."

"How can you be certain the fall was accidental?" Rose questioned as she saw her husband smiling out of the corner of her eye.

"Mrs. McClain, you can speculate as much as you want about what happened to her last night, but based on the facts we have, the coroner had no choice but to rule her death accidental. The railing next to the basement stairs was loose; the light above was dim; the wooden stairs were narrow and steep, and all three siblings swore that they left the theatre together immediately after the meeting."

"Did you give them polygraph tests?"

"Oh, Mrs. McClain, you watch too many Datelines. Polygraph tests are voluntary and are only given by police when someone is suspected of a crime. There was no reason to think that Ms. Landers' death was anything other than accidental. Besides, the tests are unreliable and not admissible in court."

"So that's it?" Rose asked in a last attempt to continue the investigation. "You're just giving up? You're going to let the Landers siblings get away with murder?"

"Look, Mrs. McClain. I don't know why you're so interested in this case or why you seemed to think Ms. Landers was murdered even though all the evidence points to an accidental death, but, respectfully, I'm getting a little irritated at your tone. In 33 years on the force, I've never let anyone get away with murder. The fact is that Ms. Landers' death was accidental, and there is absolutely no evidence to the contrary. Now, both of you have taken up enough of my time. You need to leave."

"One last question, detective." Booger chimed in for the first time. "Where is Diane Landers' body now?"

"At the funeral home, I believe."

"Which funeral home?"

"Lohmeyer."

"Thanks, detective."

Rose McClain was already out the door when her husband stood up and began to leave. She was pissed, and Booger knew it. Her friend was dead and died suspiciously, and the police were absolutely no help. And, to top it all off, she was damp, and her hair was a mess.

Booger couldn't help but smile. He loved his wife when she was worked up about a case. That was when she did her best work and was full of determination and passion. It would also help her forget about Booger leaving the top down too long and her getting soaked as a result.

"Where to?" Booger asked as he started and then revved the engine of his vintage Corvette.

"You know where to," she said, flatly.

"To the funeral home?"

"Damn right. And don't think I've forgotten about you getting me soaking wet."

"Yes, dear."

"Bufford McClain, why were you so quiet in there? You didn't ask a damn question of that detective."

"I was having fun watching you ask the questions."

Rose shot her husband a nasty look.

The rain had slowed to a drizzle when the red Corvette pulled into the parking lot of the Herman H. Lohmeyer Funeral Home. The lot was completely empty except for a black hearse parked under a canopy.

"I guess word hasn't gotten out that Lohmeyer puts the fun in funeral?" Booger said, hoping to generate a smile from his wife. It didn't work.

The detective parked the car and followed his wife into the lobby of the funeral home.

"We'd like to speak to Herman Lohmeyer, please," Rose said to a receptionist at the front desk.

The young, slender lady with short, curly brown hair and glasses that looked a little big, given her narrow-framed face, looked confused.

"I'm sorry, ma'am. Mr. Lohmeyer doesn't own the funeral home anymore. Besides, he died way before I was born."

"Well, who owns the funeral home now?"

"The Wunderlichs own it now."

"Well, could I speak to them?"

"Mrs. Wunderlich is not in, but Mr. Wunderlich is."

"OK, can I speak to him?"

"Just a second. Let me see if he's available," the receptionist said as she got up and walked down a hallway toward a large office.

A couple of minutes later, she walked back with a distinguished middle-aged gentleman in a dark blue suit next to her.

"Hello, I'm Paul Wunderlich," the man said with a smile, holding out his hand to shake.

"Yes," Rose said. "We'd like to see one of your customers, Ms. Diane Landers."

"Are you a friend or family?"

"Friend."

"I'm sorry. I didn't catch your name."

"Rose McClain, and this is my husband, Buford."

"It's certainly nice to meet you, Mr. and Mrs. McClain. But I'm afraid if you want to see Ms. Landers, you're a little too late."

"What do you mean? Did she decide not to stay?" Booger said, trying to lighten the mood. His humor fell short, and his wife nudged him in his side with her elbow.

"No. I mean, Ms. Landers has already been cremated."

"What? Who asked for her to be cremated?" Rose said in an angry voice.

"Her family, of course. They were rather insistent that she be cremated right away and her ashes disposed of."

"Her family?"

"Yes, Cornilus Landers. He and his brother and sister were Ms. Landers' only living relatives."

"How about a memorial service?"

"Afraid not. Mr. Landers was insistent that her ashes be disposed of and that there not be any type of service."

"How about the body? Was there anything odd or suspicious about it?" Rose asked.

"I'm not sure I understand."

"Well, she supposedly died from a fall down the stairs. Was there anything about her body that was inconsistent with that?"

"No, of course not. Look, Mrs. McClain, I shouldn't even be discussing this with you. You're not a relative. Please, if there is nothing else, I need to get back to work."

"No, I guess not. Thanks for your time, Mr. Wunderlich." Booger said, grabbing his wife's hand to lead her out.

"What do you think you're doing, practically dragging me out of that place, Bufford T. McClain?" Rose said as he opened the car door for her.

"Listen, sweetie. That man had no more information to give us, and quite frankly, I think he wanted you, I mean us, to leave."

"Don't 'sweetie' me. You were of no help in there. You didn't ask one question."

"I didn't need to. You were doing a fine job on your own."

Rose shot her husband another nasty look.

"Sweetie, I mean honey, what do you say we head over to the Walnut Street Inn and start our mini vacation?"

"Honestly, Buford, sometimes I just don't understand you. How can you possibly think I'm in the mood for a haunted tour vacation when my best friend was just murdered?"

"Well, darling, it will help you relax, and we can spend some quality time together."

"Quality time? Staying in a haunted bed and breakfast? Possibly seeing ghosts or spirits or whatever you want to call them. Is that your brand of fun?"

"Well, kind of. But focus on the quality alone time with me."

"No, I don't think so. I can have that same quality, alone time at home."

"Yeah, getting up early to make me breakfast, cleaning the house, going to work in the office, making me lunch and dinner, and massaging my feet?"

"I never messaged your feet. You know they creep me out."

"Well, a man can dream, can't he?"

Rose shot her husband a look that could have killed him.

"OK, seriously, Rose, I don't mean to make light of the situation. I know that you're upset. And I get it. This was someone you were beginning to get really close to. The truth is this: I had a weird dream about your friend being in the basement of the theater, and I can't quite shake it. That's what made me want to plan this mini-vacation. I can't explain it, but I had a weird dream, and I knew somehow that things had gone terribly wrong for your friend, and now that we know I was right, I feel like we really have to get to the bottom of this," he said, watching his wife's reaction closely. She had been on the verge of tears, but seemed to be calming down the more he spoke. "Plus, we can eat out every day; there would be no cleaning or work; you can sleep in if you want. And besides, the Walnut Inn is close to the Landers Theatre, and I heard that Ida and Brandon Landers have recently taken up residency there. We could keep an eye on them and take late-night strolls to the Landers Theatre. Maybe sneak inside and do a little investigating."

"How do you know Ida and Brandon Landers are staying there?"

"I know the owners of the Walnut Street Inn, Bob and Cindy Williams. I did a little investigating for them a few years back when their daughter Shelly ran off with a paroled carnival worker. They told me the two Landers siblings had been staying there while their family mansion was being renovated."

"What about Cornilus? Didn't he live there too?"

"I don't know where Cornilus is staying, but he's not at the Walnut Inn."

"OK, Booger McClain. But this vacation isn't going to be over until we know exactly what happened to Diane."

CHAPTER EIGHT
THE DINNER PARTY

It was early that evening when the red Corvette pulled up to the Walnut Street Inn. The rain had slowed to a sprinkle, and the temperature had dropped at least ten degrees.

Rose attempted to puff up her hair that had wilted in the rain while her husband grabbed the bags from the back seat and carried them up the steps to the gray wooden porch and the front door. When Booger and Rose arrived at the Walnut Street Inn, the front door was locked, and no one could be seen behind the register.

"How are we supposed to get in?" Rose asked.

"Well, I called ahead to tell them that we'd be checking in a bit late, but I don't see an envelope with our name anywhere on the porch. Maybe I misunderstood," Booger responded.

"You see, this is why I didn't want to do this. Now, we are standing out here like fools."

"It's no big deal, Sweetie. I'll just call the office."

While Booger called to talk to the manager, Rose started walking around the porch to see if she could see anyone inside. The wind came with a touch of cold and the smell of rain. Rose could see the old-growth trees on the property begin to sway and creak in the breeze. The focal point of the inn was the spacious, multi-storied old house at the corner of Walnut and John Q. Hammons Parkway. It had a strong Victorian look to it that Rose found both a bit creepy and fancy. In the back was an additional building, newer and not as grand but with the same Victorian style. With Booger still in earshot, his wife rounded the side of the main house and noticed what appeared to be a man staring at her from the porch of the second property forty feet away.

"Hello," Rose yelled, waving her hand. The man did not respond.

The older gentleman with short, wavy gray hair and beard didn't appear to be doing anything but looking at the detective, and Rose was focused on him. *"Why is this guy just standing at the door and looking out at me?"* she wondered.

Then, Booger yelled, "Honey. Where are you?"

Rose returned to the front of the Victorian house. "I'm here."

"The manager will be here in just a minute. He was very apologetic."

"Well, he ought to be. We will end up like old wet dogs out here."

Rose turned one last time to see if the man inside the inn was still watching, but he had disappeared.

"Within a minute, a young twenty-something man came from the back of the property with a humbled and hurried look. "I'm so sorry about this. I hope I didn't keep you two waiting for too long."

"No, it's no trouble at all," Rose insisted, and then she looked at Booger with narrowed eyes.

"Please come in," the host said. "I've left your keys just behind the desk. I knew you were coming a bit after our typical check-in hours, but I had planned on being at the desk when you arrived. Here are your keys, and I insist that you take a bottle of wine for your trouble. White wine or red? We have a nice pinot noir as well."

"Oh, well, if you insist, we'll take red," Rose said with a bright smile she shared with her husband, who tried not to look impressed.

"Have you two ever stayed at the Walnut Street Inn before?"

"No," Rose said. "It's our first time."

"Lovely. Well, my name is Randolph. If you need anything at all, you can call the same number you dialed before. Dinner is at 7 pm, so you have plenty of time to relax and freshen. You'll meet Bob and Cindy Williams, the owners, at dinner tonight, along with our other guests. And you're in for a treat. Mrs. Williams is making her special recipe meatloaf, mashed potatoes and brown gravy, fresh sweet corn, and homemade apple pie."

"I thought this was a Bed and Breakfast?"

"It is," Rudolph replied.

"Then why dinner, too?"

"Oh, I see what you mean, Mr. McClain. This is a special night, a meet and greet night, Mrs. Williams calls it. Mr. Williams' brother and sister-in-law are up for a visit from St. Louis, and well, Mrs. Williams loves to cook, so she thought we'd have a special dinner for the guests and family tonight. It's a small group. Besides Pat and Sue Williams, there's only one other couple, and you and your wife, of course. You are not obligated to join us, but we'd love you to join us for dinner. Offering you a free meal would make us feel better about leaving you out in the rain."

"Wouldn't miss it for anything," Rose said.

"And where is our room?" Booger asked curtly.

"Ah, yes. You are staying in the Machino Suite #213, which is on the second floor of the Carriage House. It was an old barn serving the main house in the second half of the nineteenth century. It's been renovated a long time ago, now, and is quite lovely."

"Oh, I thought we'd be in the main house," Booger said, sounding a bit disappointed.

"Well, I'm sorry, I guess they didn't tell you when you called to make reservations. The main Inn is undergoing some room renovations. The only rooms available are in the Carriage House."

"I see. So, the other guests are staying in the Carriage House too?"

"No, they are staying in two of the rooms that have already been renovated. I'm afraid those are the only two rooms suitable for guests at this time. You'll have the Carriage House all to yourselves."

"But what about the old man?" Rose asked.

"What old man?"

"The one on the porch of the Carriage House. I saw him a few minutes earlier."

"Oh, Mrs. McClain, you must be mistaken. You're the only ones staying in the Carriage House."

"I guess," said Rose, looking a little confused.

"Also, I forgot to tell you, since your husband said this is your second honeymoon, the Williams thought it would be nice to put a bottle of Champagne and a plate of chocolate-covered strawberries in your room. The strawberries are from our garden out back and were just picked this morning."

"Perfect, sir. We cannot wait. Thanks for your hospitality," Rose said, holding her bottle of wine proudly.

"Of course. It's my pleasure."

Just as Rose and Booger were about to leave, Bob and Cindy Williams, a vivacious gray-haired couple in their early to mid-seventies and owners of the Inn, walked in the front door carrying bags of groceries.

"Booger McClain, it is good to see you again," Bob said, patting him on the back like they were old friends. "And this must be your lovely bride."

"Hello, I'm Rose, the old man's lovely and much younger bride," she said with a smile.

Bob and Cindy both set the grocery bags down, put their arms out, and came in for a bear hug. "It's so good to finally meet you, Rose," Cindy said as if she were greeting a distant relative.

"Sorry, we couldn't greet you when you first got here this afternoon. Cindy and I were out shopping for dinner."

"Booger, old buddy, can I get you a drink?" Bob said, pointing toward the small bar directly behind the front desk.

"Sounds good. I mean, no, not right now, maybe later," Booger said, changing his mind after seeing the dirty look coming from his wife.

"Well, you two probably want to freshen up before dinner."

"Yes, that's what we want to do," Rose said, smiling at her husband and touching her slightly matted hair.

"Well, we put you lovebirds in the Machino Suite," Bob said. "It's named after my mother, Mary Machino Baczenas, and also is our honeymoon suite," Cindy added. "And, it's not just the honeymoon suite. It's also the most haunted room in the Inn. That is if you believe in ghosts."

"Great," Rose said as her smile disappeared.

"That's what your husband requested, I believe," Cindy added.

"I see," Rose said, darting a nasty look at her husband, who was trying to ignore her.

"Let's see now," Bob said, breaking what could have been an awkward silence. "We've got you down for three nights."

"Actually, Bob. We might need to extend that stay a little longer," Booger said as Rose's nasty stare reappeared.

"Oh, no problem, Booger. It's the end of our busy season, and we only have two rooms occupied. I think we can fit you in as long as you want to stay."

"Great," Rose sighed.

"The Carriage House is in the small building just behind us. Would you like me to show you to your room?" Bob asked as he handed Booger the room key.

"No, thanks, Bob. I think we'll be fine."

"Okay, dokey," Bob replied.

"Dinner's at 7. We're having meatloaf and apple pie à la mode tonight," Cindy added. "It's my mother's special recipe."

"The meatloaf or the apple pie?" Booger asked, trying again, unsuccessfully, to solicit a laugh.

"Both, actually," Cindy replied. "She was a great cook and talented baker right up to her 83rd birthday."

"Why did she stop then?" Rose asked.

"She died," Cindy added with an uncomfortable smile. "Although, I guess you could say she's still around. At least guests have reported seeing someone who looks like her."

"Oh, my," Rose replied.

"Yeah, she died right here at the Inn, in the Carriage House, actually, right in your room, 213. Of course, it wasn't a honeymoon suite back then, just a normal bedroom. She had lived in it ever since my daddy passed away."

"Oh, my goodness," Rose said. "If you don't mind me asking, how'd she die?"

"No, I don't mind. She hung herself from the ceiling fan.

Mother just couldn't seem to get over losing Daddy, and so, I suppose, she just one day decided to join him."

"Mother left me all her recipes and her wedding ring. I'm not nearly as talented as Mother in the kitchen, but I follow her recipes exactly the way she wrote them down, and, well, I guess they seem to turn out alright," Cindy said, glancing at her husband for confirmation.

"Uh-huh," Bob said with a smile. "Don't let her fool you. My wife is a great cook, every bit as good as her mother."

"Well. I'm looking forward to dinner," Rose said, smiling.

"Me too," Booger said after a jab to his side.

Then, the two of them went out the front door and around the back.

"You know, Booger, if Mama Williams makes an appearance in this room while we're here, you're going to have hell to pay when we get back home."

"Sweetie, I can't control the spirits."

Rose opened up her purse and pulled out a small but effective stun gun. "And I can't control where this stun gun decides to shoot," Rose said, pointing the stun gun toward Booger's crotch.

The sprinkle of rain had changed to random raindrops as the couple reached the small building in the back.

"This is the house where I just saw somebody looking at me, Booger," Rose said as they approached the front of the Carriage House.

"When?"

"When you were on the phone, I was checking this place out."

"Possibly another ghost? Let's get in before we get any wetter."

The detectives walked in and up the stairs to their room.

"This place is so lovely I can't stand it," Rose said, beaming. In the lobby of the Carriage House were old black-and-white pictures of people and the property, handmade rugs, and modern barn-style décor. "It's like Cracker Barrel, but fancy."

In the room itself was a book nook with an oversized chair, a gas fireplace, a large bathroom, and skylights above the bed, where flashes of lightning were beginning to appear. Everything reminded Rose of a simpler time, a time long ago when the pace of life was much slower.

After they got settled and while Rose was trying to untangle her hair, Booger said, "I wasn't going to tell you until morning, but these skylights were written about in a book I read a while back." Supposedly, people have seen ghosts materialize late at night under the glow of these windows. Is that exciting?"

"No. Not at all. It's probably just an optical illusion with light coming in from the outside into the dark room, and stop trying to scare me, Buford. Besides, I know that story isn't true because as long as I've known you, I've never once seen you read a book."

Just then, Rose heard someone enter the front of the Carriage House. She thought it might be the guy who was staring at her earlier, so Rose went to the door to their room to peer out the peephole. While she could clearly hear someone going up the creaky wooden staircase, she never saw anybody. The door to the adjacent room soon opened and shut, and the detective figured she had missed her chance.

"Rose, what are you doing?" Booger asked, seeing her look out the peephole in the door.

"Didn't you hear the front door open and footsteps?"

"No."

"Old man, remind me to get your hearing checked the next time we're at Walmart."

Booger didn't comment. His focus had turned to a table next to the bed, which sat a chilled bottle of Champagne and a silver platter of chocolate-covered strawberries.

Booger dropped the bags by the closet door, took off his shoes, and fell on the bed, grabbing a chocolate-covered strawberry.

"Aren't you going to put your clothes away first, old man?"

"Later," he replied with a yawn. "I'm going to eat some of these strawberries, then I'm going to take a little nap before dinner."

"Don't spoil your dinner."

"Impossible."

Rose opened her bags, neatly put away her clothes, and then went into the bathroom to shower, fix her hair and make-up, and change clothes. Booger, lying on his back with the stems of three chocolate-covered strawberries lying on his stomach, was snoring before she got her first bag unpacked.

Ninety minutes later, Rose was shaking her husband out of a sound sleep. "Time to get up, Booger. It's almost dinner time."

Booger rolled over on his side away from Rose in an attempt to ignore his wife. That's when his nose got a whiff of the warm apple pie through the open window about thirty feet from the main house's kitchen.

He inhaled deeply through his nose several times, trying to determine if the smell of homemade apple pie was real or just part of his dream. Finally convinced that the heavenly aroma was real and not a part of his imagination, Booger rose quickly to his feet.

"I'm starving, Rose. Let's go."

"Not so fast, old man. Don't you think you should wash up and change clothes?"

"Naugh, I think I'm good to go."

Rose darted a disapproving look in his direction.

"OK, maybe just a quick shower," Booger replied as Rose shook her head in agreement.

"And a shave and change of clothes," Rose replied.

"OK," Booger said in the soft voice of a child made to do something he really didn't want to do.

Booger went to his luggage, unzipped the top, and pulled out the first shirt and pair of jeans that he saw, along with his shaving kit.

Rose, seeing his choice in clothes, said, "Booger, do you really think wearing jeans to a dinner with strangers you've never seen before is a good idea?"

"Yes."

"Buford, wear a pair of slacks and a dress shirt," Rose said in a stern voice.

"Can't, hun."

"Why not?"

"'Cause all I packed are jeans and sports shirts."

"Geez, Booger. What am I going to do with you? I should have checked your suitcase before we left the house."

Booger just smiled, walked into the bathroom, and closed the door.

Twenty minutes later, the detective had showered, shaved, and dressed and was ready to go.

Noticing his wife was wearing a beautiful red dress and had put make-up on and fixed her hair, Booger said, "Sweetie, you look beautiful."

"Thanks, old man, but I look the same as when you woke up from your nap. I would have thought you would have noticed then."

"I did, but I was so overwhelmed by the smell of that apple pie that I forgot to say anything."

"Uh-huh."

"Rose, aren't you going to comment on how I look?"

"Yes, Booger. You look," Rose struggled for the right word before finally deciding on "comfortable."

Downstairs in the dining room, Bob Williams greeted the McClains as they walked into the room. "Did you find your room comfortable?"

"Yes, great," Rose responded as Booger shook his head in agreement.

"Fine, fine. We thought you'd like privacy, so we didn't put anyone in the other rooms at Carriage House."

"Are you sure, Bob?" Rose asked with a confused look.

"Yes, absolutely. You and your wife are the only people staying in the Carriage House."

"Well, that's weird because I heard someone come in, walk up the steps, and open and shut the room next to us."

"No, it must have been the wind, Mrs. McClain. No one else is staying there."

Rose nudged Booger and whispered in his ear, "Ask for another room."

Booger ignored her.

"Let me introduce you two to our other guests," Bob said. "Everyone, this lovely couple is Booger and Rose McClain." After everyone said hello, Bob gestured to the couple on the right. "Mr. and Mrs. McClain, let me introduce you to Pat and Sue Williams. They are my brother and sister-in-law down from St. Louis for a visit."

The two men shook hands, and the women hugged.

"And over here are Brandon and Ida Landers, brother and sister, and owners of the famous Landers Theatre in Springfield.

After cordial greetings, the couples took their seats at the table.

Rose nudged her husband and whispered, "See how the others are dressed, dresses, slacks, button-down dress shirts, sports coats. Don't you feel bad that you didn't pack something a little nicer?"

"Not really," Booger responded, to which he got a nasty look from his wife.

"Mr. and Mrs. McClain, can I get you a cocktail before dinner is served?" Bob asked, pointing to the bar.

"White wine, please," Rose responded.

"And I'll take a rye whiskey, double, with one ice cube," Booger replied.

"Oh, sorry, McClain. We don't have rye whiskey. Would you settle for some fine Missouri whiskey or perhaps a good Kentucky Bourbon?"

"I didn't know any whiskey was made in Missouri," Booger responded.

"My, yes. Missouri has some fine whiskey distilleries. The one we have here is the Wood Hat Aged Blue Corn Whiskey, produced in New Florence, MO. It's 100 percent pure corn alcohol, distilled in copper kettles, and aged for over a year. Trust me, it packs quite a punch."

"Sounds good to me. Make me a double with two ice cubes," Booger responded as Rose jabbed him in the side. "Better make that a single, Bob, and forget the two ice cubes."

"By the way, where's your lovely wife, Bob?" Rose asked.

"In the kitchen, just finishing up with dinner. She'll be here in a few minutes."

Rose and Booger sat down next to Pat and Sue Williams and directly across from Brandon and Ida Landers.

"What part of St. Louis do you and your wife live in, Mr. Williams?"

"Please call me Pat, and you can call my wife, Sue, or Snickers if you want. That's her nickname."

"OK, Pat, and please call us Booger and Rose, or you can call my wife "thorny" if you want. That's her nickname."

Rose, not so gently, kicked her husband in the shin.

"So, Pat and Sue, what part of St. Louis do you live in?"

"Festus, actually. It's about 30 miles south of St. Louis."

"Nice. So, how long are you visiting?"

"No real set amount of time, Booger. My wife and I are retired and have been for about five years now. Our kids are grown and live a ways away, so we just thought it would be fun to come down and visit my big brother and his wife. We'll probably stay until they kick us out, Pat said with a laugh.

His wife, Sue, chimed in with a sort of prolonged high-pitched giggle that instantly defined how she got the nickname "Snickers."

Rose looked over at Bob to see that he was not nearly as amused by his brother's comment.

Rose then turned her attention to the Landers' siblings. "So, you two own the Landers Theatre?"

"Yes," Brandon responded. "Well, actually, we own it with our other brother, Cornilus. All three of us inherited it from our parents years ago."

"Well, that's quite a theatre," Booger added.

"Oh, have you been there, Mr. McClain?" Brandon asked.

"Please call me Booger, and no, I haven't been there, but I've lived in Springfield a lot of years, and I'm very aware of its reputation."

"Reputation? Mr. McClain. I mean Booger."

"Well, what I mean is, it has got a reputation for being one of the most haunted places in Springfield."

"Oh yes, you're right. But honestly, I can say that in the time my brother, sister, and I have owned the place, we have yet to see a ghost or spirit or really anything out of the ordinary."

"But there have been sightings over the years, and I believe several unusual deaths in the theatre," Rose commented.

"Yes, but nothing like that for quite a few years."

"With the exception of last night?" Rose asked.

"Oh, I see you've heard the news today," Brandon replied. "A tragic accident, I'm afraid. That poor lady simply tripped going down those stairs. I told Cornilus just the other day that we need to replace those stairs and get better lighting in the basement."

"Yes, what was the poor lady's name?" Rose asked as Booger tapped gently on her foot in an attempt to get his wife to change the conversation.

"Diane Landers," Brandon replied.

"Yes, a relative of yours?"

"She was our niece. We weren't very close, I'm afraid. She had a rather ominous past, living in an orphanage after her parents died. She had some psychological problems too, I'm afraid. Tragic life."

"So, what happened. All the news said was that she fell down the stairs and broke her neck," Rose said as Booger again stepped on her foot in an attempt to slow down the speed of their conversation. He wanted his wife to get answers, but he didn't want to interrogate the Landers the second they met them.

"I'm afraid that's all we know, too," Brandon replied, glancing toward his sister.

"But why was she there alone so late at night?" Rose asked with Booger jabbing her side.

"Well, she really wasn't, not for very long anyway. She was also part owner of the Landers Theatre, a gift she inherited from her parents. She was there meeting with Cornilus, Ida, and me to discuss business."

"Why so late at night?"

"You've never been in the theatre business before, have you, Mrs. McClain?"

"No."

"Well, I'm afraid performances and rehearsals go well into the night, so the only quiet time to meet is after everyone else has left."

"I see. So, were you or your siblings present when the accident happened?"

"Afraid not. We left immediately after the meeting. Ms. Landers stayed behind to take care of some things in the office. That office was downstairs in the basement. I suppose she must have fallen on her way down to it."

"I see. So, no one was there?"

"No, the cleaning staff found her this morning. There was nothing anyone could do."

An awkward silence followed that statement, but it was broken shortly by Bob returning with a glass of Chablis for Rose and a glass of whiskey for Booger.

"Well, thanks, Bob," Booger said, raising his glass to toast everyone at the table.

"To current friends and new friends," Booger toasted and

then took a large sip of the Missouri Whiskey. It hit his tongue smoothly but encountered his taste buds like a bull in a China shop. It was with great concentration that he was able to swallow the horrid concoction. He didn't know if it was the blue corn whiskey or the year of aging in a plywood barrel that gave it a kick that sent his taste buds into a full revolt. Whatever it was, he wasn't going to tempt fate again with a second swallow.

Luckily, he didn't need to. Cindy Williams entered the room carrying a large plate of meatloaf. "Hi, everyone, dinner is ready."

Bob followed behind with a large bowl of mashed potatoes, brown gravy, sweet corn, and homemade biscuits.

Few words were said during dinner, partly because the food was so good that everyone's mouths remained full and partly because there was tension in the room after the conversation about Diane's death.

Rose spent much of the dinner glancing across the table at Brandon and Ida. The brother and sister were whispering to each other throughout most of the dinner. Rose tried desperately to hear what they were saying, but she couldn't make out anything. Booger ignored everyone, cleaned one plate, and went for seconds and thirds.

Cindy, who was seated next to him, looked over at him in amazement as he wolfed down plate after plate of food. "It's good to see a man with a hearty appetite," she said.

"Pretty soon, it's going to be a fat man with a clotted artery," Rose shot back in a low voice that only her husband could hear.

"What did you say, Mrs. McClain?" Cindy asked.

"I said, sweetie, you need to save room for the homemade apple pie."

"My yes, my sister-in-law makes wonderful pies," Cindy replied.

After the dinner plates were cleared, coffee and after-dinner cordials of Grand Marnier, Sherry, and Kahlua were offered. Booger took coffee and Kahlua. Rose opted for sherry.

A short time later, warm apple pie with homemade cinnamon ice cream was served to everyone.

Booger cleaned his plate in record time, then sat back, closed his eyes, and patted his stomach.

"I'm ready for a nap, Rose," he said.

"You're ready for a triple bypass," Rose shot back.

Booger, eyeing his wife barely touching her dessert, said, "Rose, are you going to finish that? If not, can I have the rest?"

Rose looked over at her husband's hungry eyes, smiled, and said, "No, and no."

After dinner, everyone retired to the bar for a nightcap before bed.

Cindy grabbed four wine glasses and a bottle of Chardonnay and led the women to a table just outside the bar area.

Bob took his position behind the bar, pulled out a nearly full bottle of Wood Hat Aged Blue Corn Whiskey, and poured a glass for Pat and Brandon. "Care for another glass of this fine Missouri whiskey?" Bob asked, smiling at Booger.

"No, no. It's wonderful stuff, Bob, but I think one glass is enough. How about some of that great Kentucky bourbon you were talking about?

"Absolutely, buddy," Bob said, reaching behind the bar for a bottle of Buffalo Trace bourbon.

"I've never heard of that bourbon, Bob. Where'd you find it?"

"You know, Booger, it's funny. I had never heard of it either until the wife and I took a vacation to Kentucky to travel the whiskey trail to visit all the best distilleries."

"So, Buffalo Trace was on the whiskey trail?"

"No, it wasn't. The wife and I got lost, wandered off the trail by a few miles, and found the Buffalo Trail Distillery purely by accident."

"Lucky you."

"Yes, exactly. It turned out to be the best bourbon I've ever had. And, you know what, it's relatively cheap for the quality. You can actually find it in almost any liquor store now because it's affordable, about half the price of the better-known, pricey stuff."

"You don't say, Bob. I can't wait to taste it. Why don't you pour me a glass with three ice cubes."

Bob did and then poured himself a glass.

"Here's to the best cheap bourbon in Kentucky," Bob said, lifting his glass.

Booger closed his eyes, prepared his taste buds for another assault, and took a big sip. A few seconds later, a huge smile appeared on his face. It was as if he had just seen his family in Heaven again.

"By God, Bob. You're right. This is the best bourbon I've ever had."

It was a shock to his taste buds, a heavenly taste that transformed everything he had ever thought about bourbons before.

Bob reached behind the bar and pulled out four cigars. "Care for a stogie, gentleman?"

"Absolutely," they all replied almost in unison.

Bob handed each man a cigar. Booger looked his over, then

closed his eyes and smelled it. The aroma was wonderful. The cigar was thick with a golden sleeve that read, "Cuban Golden."

"Did you get these from Cuba, Bob?"

"A few years back, I think Obama was President, Americans were allowed to travel to Cuba. So, the wife and I booked a small cruise ship departing out of Miami and took a trip to Havana. Damn, that city was beautiful but old. Everything was old. Every car we saw was from the fifties, it seemed like. Anyway, we found this tiny bar away from the touristy area. The aroma of fine tobacco was everywhere in that bar and even outside it. It was such a heavenly aroma that I just had to try a cigar. It just so happened that a young lady in the bar was selling them, so I bought one, lit it, and my God, it was the best-tasting cigar I had ever had."

"So, you brought some back to the States?"

"Nah. I wanted to, but Customs wouldn't allow us to bring them back."

"So, how'd you do it?" Booger asked.

"I didn't. On the way back, the wife and I befriended an elderly couple from the Villages in central Florida. They tried to talk us into retiring there. They got some sort of gift card or something for referring people. But the wife and I weren't interested. Too damn hot there, you know, and the bugs and alligators. No sir-re, give me Missouri anytime over that. Long story short, Elmer and Gladys, that was the couple's names, knew an ex-Cuban out of Miami who knew someone else who sold Cuban knock-off cigars. We had to go to a kind of seedy part of Miami to find him, but it was worth it. He sold me a box, and every month now, I get another box from him. They're expensive, and I have to pay cash and wire the money to him first, but they're worth it."

Booger lit his cigar and took a long, deep drag. Then, his eyes seemed to bulge, and he began to sweat. His taste buds were in full revolt again. He quickly dropped the cigar in an ashtray and took a large gulp of his Buffalo Trace bourbon to drive out the poison. After that, Booger was convinced that Bob may have a knack for finding good bourbon but had absolutely no taste in cigars or whiskey.

Booger turned his head to see Pat and Brandon smoking the horrid cigars and drinking the gut-wrenching whiskey with pure enjoyment.

"Can I have another Blue Corn Whiskey, brother?" Pat said, holding his empty glass out.

"Me too," chimed in Brandon.

"Enjoying those cigars and whiskey, boys?" Booger said in amazement.

"Best damn Missouri whiskey I've ever had," Pat replied.

"Yeah, and the Cuban cigars are incredible, too," Brandon added.

"Not Cuban," Bob injected. "Cuban knockoffs."

The conversation was lively at the women's table, too, at least between Cindy, Sue, and Rose. Ida barely said a word and did that only when asked a direct question.

"You know, ladies, Pat and I almost got a divorce," Sue offered after her third glass of Chardonnay."

"What? You never told me that, Sue."

"My yes, I'd had enough, and one day I just gave him an ultimatum. He had to make a choice. It was either fantasy football or me."

"So, he chose you?" Cindy asked.

"No. But he did buy me a new diamond necklace."

The women chuckled, all except Ida. She seemed to have

other things on her mind.

Then, the conversation turned to Rose.

"Did Booger ever mention that he helped Bob and me out a long time ago?"

"Yes," Rose answered reluctantly, hoping that that would end the conversation and that Cindy would change the subject. She didn't.

"Yeah, oh, it must be fifteen years or so now. We were having a little problem with our daughter. She had fallen for this guy who came to town with one of those traveling carnivals. Scary looking guy, maybe twenty years older than my teenage daughter. Shaggy, long, dirty blond hair, big scar on his right cheek, tattoos all over his body. Turned out that he'd just got out of prison. Well, Bob grounded her and forbade her from seeing the guy again. That only made her more determined to see him. She climbed out the window the night the carnival was leaving town and went to be with him. She just got up and disappeared. We didn't hear from her and had no idea where she was. That's when we hired your husband to find her. Booger is quite a detective."

That was when Ida perked up.

"It was about three weeks, but your husband finally found her and brought her back to us."

"So, everything is fine with your daughter now?" Rose asked.

"Well, no, not exactly. Turned out my little Josey was pregnant. Twins actually. She gave birth right here."

"In Springfield?" Rose asked.

"No, right here in this bar, on the very table we are sitting."

"My," Rose exclaimed.

"Yeah, my Josey popped those two kids out before Bob

could even warm up the car. Two months later, Josey and those two boys were gone."

"Died?"

"No, just up and disappeared. Turned out my Josey had been writing to a guy in the prison in Jeff City. She had fallen in love again. I heard that they were married in a prison service two weeks later. I haven't heard from her since."

That was when Ida spoke up, "So your husband is a police detective?" she asked, looking at Rose.

"No, he's a private detective, retired now," Rose added.

"Oh girl," Cindy added. "Booger's not the only detective in the family. Rose is one, too, I'm told. She and Booger have been on the news and in the papers for solving some high-profile crimes in the past."

Ida's face turned pale, and she said, "I'm sorry, ladies. I'm not feeling so good. I think it's time to go to bed."

"Oh dear," Cindy said, "You know what helps me is a hot tea with honey. Want me to make one for you and bring it up?"

"No, thanks. I really just think I need a good night's sleep."

With that, she stood up, went over to her brother, and whispered in his ear. Brandon excused himself, saying, "Gentleman, sorry to break this up, but I believe it's our bedtime. My sister and I are going to call it a night."

"It's late for us, too," Rose said. I think Booger and I will head on to bed also."

"Right after I finish this fine Kentucky bourbon."

"No, now, Booger."

Booger took a big sip and stood up. "See everyone in the morning. By the way, Cindy, what's for breakfast?"

"Fluffy lemon-blueberry pancakes, thick-cut farm-fresh hickory-smoked bacon, and fresh fruit."

"I'll be the first down."

"Careful, old man," Rose said softly. "You don't want to trip on your own tongue."

CHAPTER NINE
A HAUNTING AT THE INN

Booger was ready for bed as soon as he got back to his room that night. His wife was not.

After changing into her night clothes, Rose joined her husband in bed. Booger was sound asleep and snoring.

"Wake up, Booger. We need to talk," she said, shaking her husband.

When the shaking did no good. Rose resorted to poking her husband in the ribs. That worked. Booger slowly came out of dead sleep to say in a groggy voice, "Honey, can't we talk in the morning. I'm exhausted."

"Well, if you don't care that I can't sleep until I get some things off my mind, then I guess so."

"Thanks, honey," Booger said, going back to sleep.

"Buford T. McClain," she yelled, jabbing her husband in the ribs again. "We're going to talk whether you want to or not."

"Yes, dear," he said, rubbing his eyes before sitting up.

"Did you notice that Ida barely said a word?"

"So? Some people aren't as social as others."

"No, that's not it. She was worried. Actually, she was afraid, I think. Her hand was shaking at dinner when she tried to get some food with her fork, and she stared down a lot. I think her mind was somewhere else and not on the conversation at the dinner. She was the same way when the girls had drinks. That was until Cindy brought up the fact that you and I are private detectives. I think knowledge of that frightened her. She seemed to get anxious and soon after said she wasn't feeling well and needed to go to bed."

"Maybe she didn't feel well, Rose."

"No, I don't think that was it because soon after, she went over and whispered something in her brother's ear, and they both headed upstairs. And don't you think it's odd that both of them are sleeping in the same bedroom? I mean, I would think a brother and sister would have separate rooms."

"Maybe there are two beds in their room, Rose. Maybe they've got things to discuss that they don't want others to hear. I mean, one or more of those siblings must have killed your friend. I'm sure conversations about that would be something you wouldn't want others to hear."

"Yeah, I suppose. Which brings up another question. Where is Cornilus, and why isn't he staying at the Inn, too?"

"Maybe there wasn't enough room in the bed."

"What was Brandon like?" Rose asked, ignoring Booger's attempt at humor.

"He seemed nice. Except he had absolutely no taste when it came to whiskey and cigars."

"OK. I meant, did he say anything about the death of Diane, or talk about his brother or sister, or maybe talk about what happened last night?"

"No."

"Well, you're a big help, old man. What did you do? Just drink and smoke and ignore everything else that happened around you."

"I didn't really smoke. The cigars that Bob handed out were terrible."

"What am I going to do with you, Booger McClain?"

"I've got a couple of ideas. Why don't you roll over here, and I'll whisper them in your ear."

"You wish. Go to sleep, Oldie McFoldie."

It was a restless sleep for Booger. Funny how you can be sound asleep, snoring away, deep into a dream, then suddenly woken up by your wife, and after that, you can't seem to get back into that sound sleep. It was like that for Booger that night. He tried numerous times to latch onto a dream that would carry him through the night, but it just didn't happen. Rose, on the other hand, had no trouble falling into a dream and off into a deep sleep.

When he finally did manage to dream, it was a nightmare. The man with the kangaroo tail was back. He entered the room through the door, not opening it, just floating right through it. Booger tried to keep his eyes closed, to not look at him. But it was no use. As hard as he tried to keep them closed, some unnatural force kept pushing his eyelids up until finally, they locked in place, and they were impossible to close.

The kangaroo man, mostly a man with a long, white beard and large green eyes but with the tail of a kangaroo, was looking directly into Booger's face. Its face was familiar. The creature looked like Samuel, but Booger couldn't be sure. *Are there other kangaroo men, or is there only Samuel?* Booger wondered. It hopped onto Rose's stomach, although Rose didn't wake up or even flinch. Then he moved slowly up her until it/he, whatever it was, just a few inches from Booger's face. Frightened and confused, not knowing if this was a dream or real, Booger tried to look away, but some force was making it impossible to turn his head or close his eyes.

The kangaroo man was standing on Rose's head now, yet

she didn't wake up. His teeth were large and sharp, almost like the blade of a knife. Inches away from the detective and leering over him, the kangaroo man began to laugh – a dark, haunting laugh that was somehow a combination of a grunt and a deep, sadistic chuckle.

The odor of the kangaroo man was horrid, and Booger tried desperately to hold his breath. It was a smell, much like a decaying corpse, a smell that Booger had known a half-dozen times in his life and one that he would never forget.

When the laughter stopped, the kangaroo man spoke. "Darkness below, death above, disappearing love. Time to run."

Then, the kangaroo man simply vanished as Booger watched helplessly. The traumatic experience was enough of a jolt to wake the detective, but the lingering feeling it left in its wake was enough to make the detective wonder if he had been asleep at all for the encounter.

"Rose, Rose, wake up."

"No, I want to sleep," she barely managed to say.

"Wake up, Rose. I need to talk to you."

"If you wake me up, old man, my stun gun is going to do more than point at your sensitive area."

"OK, dear. We'll talk in the morning."

"Good choice."

It was 3 am. Booger was up for good. He quietly got out of bed, went into the bathroom, and wiped water over his eyes. Then he heard it.

The front door to the Carriage House opened and shut. Footsteps were heard walking slowly up the stairs. Booger hurried over to the front door of the room. He held his right eye against the peephole. It was a narrow view, but it showed the area just beyond the top of the stairs.

As the footsteps got closer, he focused all of his attention on that small area just beyond the final step. A few seconds later, he could see a boot step into the bottom of his vision. Then a second boot, a dirty boot, a working boot. Old, tattered, and worn jeans came into view. No, it was overalls. Finally, the face of an old man, wrinkled, worn, short, thinning gray hair, and dark eyes that reminded Booger of how a body looks when the person has been dead for some time and died with their eyes open. The eyes seemed hollow and stared mindlessly at the wall ahead of him. He had a blank look with absolutely no expression on his face. It was as if Booger was looking at a walking corpse. So much so that it sent chills down his back.

The man walked down the hallway to room 215, directly next to Booger and Rose's room. He opened the door and walked in.

Booger quickly changed out of his pajamas and into his jeans and shirt, opened the room door quietly, and walked in his socks so as not to make noise a few feet down the hallway.

At door 215, Booger heard a conversation going on inside the room, a man and a woman, he thought, although they spoke softly, so the conversation was impossible to understand.

Booger placed his eye directly in front of the peephole, hoping he could see inside. But he couldn't. The peephole only worked on the inside of the room.

So, he quietly laid down on the hallway carpet. There was a narrow gap between the floor and the bottom of the door. He maneuvered sideways so his right eye could get a view underneath the door of room 215. Finally, something came into focus. At first, it was impossible to know exactly what it was. Then the object moved back just slightly, and Booger quickly jumped to his feet.

What he saw was a woman's slipper pointed directly at the door, directly behind the door. He knew then that the woman on the other side was staring out the peephole at him.

Booger hurried back to his room and shut the door. Rose was still sound asleep. He sat in a rocking chair in the corner of the room, rocking back and forth as he drank a glass of water, trying to settle his nerves.

Suddenly, he heard the door of room 215 close and footsteps moving down the hall. Booger got to his feet and went to the peephole in his door. When he looked out, two dark eyes were looking directly back at him through the peephole. Booger jumped backwards, hitting a table and falling to the floor.

The crashing noise woke Rose up. "Booger McClain, what in the world are you doing lying flat on the floor?"

"Nothing, Rose, go back to sleep."

Booger spent what was left of the night in the rocking chair, waiting for the sun to come up.

He had just dozed off in that chair when the smell of bacon frying through the open window woke him back up.

"Rose, breakfast is cooking. Time to get up," he said, shaking her awake.

"Unless you want 10,000 volts of electrical current to be shot into your testicles, McClain, you better stop shaking me."

Booger backed off and sat in the chair to wait for his wife to wake up naturally.

Thirty minutes later, they were dressed and walking to the Inn for breakfast.

"Rose, smell that bacon and those blueberry pancakes," he said, inhaling deeply.

"Lemon-blueberry," Rose corrected.

"Rose, that smells like thick-sliced hickory bacon with a

touch of brown sugar. My mouth is watering."

"Does your sense of smell work for anything other than food?"

"I don't know. I never thought about it."

"Well, something outside our door was giving off a horrible odor when we left this morning."

"So, you smelled it too, Rose?"

Yes, just as we left the room. It only lasted for a couple of seconds and was gone. I didn't say anything because I thought it was you, considering everything you ate at dinner last night, I kind of expected some stomach issues from you. But the more I think about it, that smell was different."

"Like a corpse that's been sitting out in the sun for a few days?"

"McClain, what makes you think I ever took a whiff of a corpse that had been lying in the sun for a few days?"

"Well, have you?"

"No."

"Well, I have, and trust me, that's what it smelled like."

Booger and Rose walked in the front door to the inn, and Booger immediately darted for the pot of fresh coffee that was steaming on a coffee bar just outside the dining room. He filled a cup with the dark roast, closed his eyes as he sniffed the heavenly smell, and then took a sip.

"Folgers," he exclaimed in excitement to Rose. "All the best places have Folgers."

"Is it as good as mine?" Rose asked.

"No, dear," Booger said after considering his answer carefully. "But it's Folgers."

Booger and Rose were the first of the couples to arrive for breakfast. Bob was setting up the table while his wife Cindy, was busy in the kitchen. Booger took his coffee and moved just outside the kitchen to smell the aroma. There were few things in the world that Booger McClain loved more than thick-cut hickory bacon hot off the frying pan. Add a touch of brown sugar to that, and you'd better keep your hands away when that plate of bacon is set in front of the detective.

"Bob, you are a lucky man. Your wife is a great cook."

"Thanks, buddy."

Rose shot a disconcerting look at her husband. Booger, seeing the look, added, "And I'm a lucky man, too. Rose is an outstanding cook."

Rose's frown turned to a smile.

Letting her coffee cool for just a couple of minutes, Rose took her first sip. Her taste buds were in heaven. The coffee was Folgers, alright, hearty, dark roast coffee with a distinctive flavor, but this coffee was like no other Folgers Rose had ever had. She couldn't place what it was, but Cindy had doctored up this coffee someway. Definitely, there was a touch of cinnamon, but there was something else also, or perhaps a combination of other spices. "*Nutmeg,*" she wondered. "*Perhaps vanilla, ginger, or lavender syrup.*" Rose couldn't place it. She took a second sip and whispered under her breath, "I hate her."

The silence was broken when the other two couples walked down the steps from the second floor.

"Good morning," Cindy yelled out.

"Good morning," everyone replied.

"My goodness, I had a great night's sleep," Sue announced. "That bed was so comfortable, and the ceiling fan was wonderful. I slept so well that I didn't even hear my husband snoring, and if you ever heard him snore, you'd know that was quite an accomplishment. Pat sounds a little bit like a jet engine revving itself for takeoff."

Pat smiled and declared, "I need some caffeine. Where's the coffee?"

Bob pointed to the coffee bar. "Over their little brother."

"Bob, you got any hot tea. Maybe Chamomile or a good Herbal?" Sue asked.

"Yeah, Sue. We've got a variety of tea bags at the coffee bar. I'll get you a cup of hot water."

"Could you get one for me, too, if it's not too much trouble?" Ida asked.

"Certainly," Bob responded as he walked into the kitchen.

Brandon smiled and walked over to the bar, filled a cup three-quarters of the way with the joe, then added half and half and two cubes of sugar.

"Mr. Landers, how are you doing this morning?" Booger asked as he made his way over to the coffee bar to pour a second cup.

"Fine, thanks, Mr. …"

"McClain. But just call me Booger."

"Unusual name."

"Yes, nickname, actually. Buford is my actual name, but everyone calls me Booger."

"You're a detective, right?"

"Yeah, private detective."

"Here on business or pleasure?"

"For my wife's pleasure, actually. She loves these quaint bed and breakfasts."

"You live in Springfield, right?"

"Yes, just a few miles away."

"Why'd you come here? What I mean is if you're on vacation, I'd think you'd want to get away from home."

"You'd think, but this is where Rose wanted to come. She's never been here before."

It was then that Bob came out of the kitchen carrying two cups of hot water, which he handed to Sue and Ida, then announced, "Let's all sit down. Breakfast is ready."

Bob returned to the kitchen, and a short time later, he and Cindy came out carrying a plate of large, fluffy lemon-blueberry pancakes, a large platter of thick bacon, and a large bowl of mixed fruit.

Booger inhaled deeply as the platter of bacon was put down directly in front of him. After Cindy said grace, the food was passed around. Booger grabbed six slices of the thick, sliced hickory-smoked bacon, and as he reached for more, Rose jabbed him in the side. "Leave some for the others, dear."

He took a similar quantity of the fluffy pancakes when they came around.

"Sweetie, you're not going to have room on that plate for fruit."

"So."

"So, take some fruit."

"OK." He said, taking one strawberry out of the bowl and onto his plate."

Booger coated all six pancakes with a generous portion of butter, and when the syrup came around, he poured it on everything, bacon and strawberry included. "Real maple syrup?" he asked, smiling at Bob.

"That's right. Real sugar and everything."

"Oh, yes," Booger whispered. Real maple syrup was his favorite, and something that Rose refused to serve him because of the large number of calories.

"Are you trying to give yourself a stroke?" Rose asked,

looking at a plate full of cholesterol.

In just a few minutes, Booger had consumed the entire plate with the exception of one lone strawberry sitting in a pond of syrup. He sat back in his chair, patted his stomach, and let out a big sigh. "Cindy, I've got to say that was one incredible breakfast."

"Well, thank you, Mr. McClain. It's a pleasure to cook for a man who appreciates food as much as you do."

Rose just shook her head.

"How'd you and your wife enjoy the room last night, Mr. McClain?"

"Rose slept just fine. I had a little trouble staying asleep, though. Bob, did you happen to rent the room next to us out last night?"

"No, you were the only ones in the Carriage House."

"That's strange because someone was in room 215 last night, an older gentleman in overalls and a woman, older too, I think, although I didn't get a good look at her."

"Must be a dream you had, old buddy, because we didn't rent that room. In fact, the only keys to that room never left the office."

"Unless..." Cindy added.

"Unless what?" Booger asked.

"Unless you saw the ghosts of Mamma and Pappa Williams."

Everyone laughed.

"Do you believe in ghosts, old buddy?" Bob asked.

"I do," Rose interrupted.

"Goodness dear, did you see the old woman and man too?" Cindy asked Rose.

"No. I didn't see or hear anyone. I slept through the night."

"Well, I suppose it could have been a dream," Booger said, knowing that no one was going to believe his story.

As the conversation turned to weather and activities planned for the day, Booger asked Brandon and Ida about the Landers Theatre.

"You know Rose and I have never been to the Landers Theatre. I hear it's a grand place. How long had it been in your family?"

Ida sat silently, choosing to let her brother answer the question. "Oh, gosh. I guess about seventy years now. It's been passed down from generation to generation. Diane, rest her soul, was the last one to own it."

"What's going to happen to it now since Miss Landers died?"

Brandon thought it over for a few seconds before answering. "Well, I guess if she had a will, it would be passed on to whoever she listed in the will, and if she didn't have a will, it will probably stay in the family."

"Meaning you and your sister will inherit it?" Booger asked.

"And Cornilus, too."

"Yes, your older brother, right?" Rose asked.

"That's right."

"Do you know if Diane Landers had a will?" Booger asked.

"No. If she did, she never mentioned it to us."

"You know, Brandon, Rose and I would love to get a tour of the old theatre. Do you provide tours?"

"Sometimes, but not very often. Normally, only for special guests or sometimes a tour group visiting."

"I don't suppose it would be possible for Rose and me to get a tour?"

"Oh my. I would need to ask Cornilus. He manages the theatre and grants special requests. Regardless, I don't think we'd be allowed to give any tours until the dust settles over Ms. Landers' death."

"Certainly, I understand."

After breakfast, Booger and Rose headed back to the Carriage House to freshen up and make plans for the day.

"Booger, did you notice that Ida didn't say a word at breakfast?"

"Maybe she's shy."

"No, I think it's more than that. She barely touched her breakfast, and her hand was shaking when she picked up her teacup. I think she's either worried or she's afraid of something, and I'd be willing to bet it has something to do with Diane's death."

"Or something to do with her big brother, Cornilus."

"Yeah, where do you think he is, Booger?"

"That's the $64,000 question."

"Sweetie, you're about 50 years behind the times. I believe it's now the million-dollar question, you know, considering inflation. No, seriously, Booger, where do you think he is?"

"Considering the visitors we had last night, I'd say he's very close."

"So, you really did see an old man and woman staying in the room next to us?"

"Yes, and the kangaroo man, too."

When Booger and Rose approached Room 213, both stopped in their tracks, and Rose gasped. Sitting outside their room were their suitcases, filled with all their clothes, folded neatly.

"What the hell?" Booger exclaimed. "Rose, did you pack

our clothes before we left for breakfast?"

"No."

When Booger got close to the door, he heard voices inside. He used his room key to open the door, and when he did, there was nobody inside. "Rose, grab your suitcase, and let's go inside."

"No way, McClain. I'm not stepping foot in that room. I think it's pretty obvious that someone doesn't want us in there."

"OK. Wait here, and I'll check it out."

Booger walked into room 213 and looked under the bed and in the bathroom. No one was there. Then he opened the closet door. Inside, two old suitcases lay on the floor, empty. And hung up in the closet were a man's and a woman's clothes. But they weren't clothes from a recent time. They were old, not worn, not tattered, but old from an earlier generation, a much earlier generation.

"Rose, you should see this," Booger said.

Reluctantly, Rose came into the room, and when she looked inside the closet, she couldn't believe her eyes. Hanging neatly in front of her were clothes that looked to be nearly a hundred years old, in excellent condition as if they had recently been purchased.

Upon further examination of the room, they discovered drawers full of clothes, underwear, pajamas, and socks, all of which looked to be from a time long ago.

"This is freaking me out, Buford. I want you to get us a different room," Rose said.

"Rose, I don't believe in ghosts."

"But I do, old man."

"OK, I'll ask for a different room, but not now. If it's not ghosts, and I don't think it is, then someone is trying to frighten us into leaving, and I want to know why. Give me a day to look into it, and if I don't find a reasonable explanation for what's going on, we'll ask for a different room."

"So, what do we do in the meantime, Booger? I don't want to stay in this room."

"Well, I don't think I'm going to get any answers before tonight. I figure whoever is doing this is done for now, but will likely come back tonight, probably late tonight when they think we're asleep. So, I suggest we get away from the inn and do something fun."

CHAPTER TEN
THE WILL

"So, what are we going to do today. Booger?"

"Whatever you want, darling."

"Well, there's a farmers' market in Nixa today and a picnic at Lake Springfield. Both of those sound good."

"Whatever you want, darling."

"We could hit a new stop on the Cashew Chicken Trail, or there's a kite festival going on at the Botanical Gardens."

"Whatever you want, dear."

"Also, there's an Art in Bloom festival. Oh, and I really think you'd like the Corndog kickoff at the Ozark Fairgrounds. Wait, Booger, on second thought, maybe we should choose something indoors."

"Why?"

"Well, it's cloudy. Don't you worry that it might rain?"

"Nah, I listened to the news this morning, and KY3 says there's less than a 10 percent chance of rain."

"Well, actually, when they say there's a 10 percent chance, that refers to the coverage area."

"Come again?"

"It means there's a good chance it'll rain, but only in 10 percent of the coverage area."

"Huh. Really?"

"Yeah, that's what I heard."

"So, maybe there's a 100 percent chance it will rain in Blue Eye and Rogersville, but a 0 percent chance it'll rain in Springfield or Branson or anywhere else in southwest Missouri?"

"Yeah, that's the idea."

"Hmm. I would prefer to go back to my old way of thinking about it."

"OK. So, does that mean you're up for doing something outdoors?"

"I am darling."

After freshening up, Booger and Rose got in the red Corvette, put the top down, and sped away.

"Where to first, sweetie?"

"Let's try the farmers' market in Nixa."

"OK, let's go pick up some farmers from the market."

A few minutes later, thunder could be heard in the distance. Then, several bolts of lightning.

"Maybe you'd better put the top up, Booger."

"Nah. There's barely a cloud in the sky."

Two minutes later, rain started pouring down without warning. No sprinkles, no light rain. It was coming down in buckets. Booger began to roll the top up as fast as he could. Rose grabbed her purse and a piece of newspaper to try to shield her hair. It was no use. "Booger, it is 100 percent raining on my head!" Without any further comments, the detective turned the car around and headed back to the Walnut Street Inn.

By the time Rose got back inside the Carriage House, her hair was soaking wet, and so were her clothes. Ten minutes later, just as Rose was blow-drying her hair, her cell phone rang.

"Can you get that, Booger?"

"Sure," he said, picking up her phone from the nightstand. "Hello, you've reached Rose McClain's answering service. How can I help you?"

"Yes, this is Attorney Mike Robinson. I need to speak to Mrs. McClain, please."

"Certainly, I'll see if she can be disturbed."

"Rose, darling, there's a lawyer on the phone who wishes to speak with you."

"OK, old man, just bring me the phone."

"Hello, this is Rose."

"Rose McClain?"

"Yes, Rose McClain."

"Mrs. McClain, this is Mike Robinson, attorney for Diane Landers. I assume you knew Ms. Landers?"

"Yes. She was a friend."

"Well, I'm not sure that you're aware, but Ms. Landers passed away a few days ago."

"Yes, I know."

"Well, Mrs. McClain. I will be reading her Will this afternoon at 2 pm, and I think you should be here."

"Why? I'm just a friend."

"Well, Mrs. McClain, I suspect that Ms. Landers thought of you as a great deal more than a friend."

"Why would you think that?"

"Because Mrs. McClain, you are the sole beneficiary of her estate."

"No. That can't be."

"Yes, it's all spelled out in her will."

"Oh my."

"Mrs. McClain, please be at my office today at 2 pm for the full details of her will."

"Of course, yes. I'll be there."

Rose walked out of the bathroom with a shocked look.

"What's the matter, honey?"

"That was the attorney for Diane Landers. I need to be at his office at 2 pm for the reading of her will."

"Why, did she leave you something?"

"Yeah, her entire estate."

"No way."

"Way."

At 1:40 pm, the detectives left the Carriage House and started walking toward their car when they heard shouting coming from the patio of the main inn. Standing on the patio were Bob Williams and Brandon Landers in a heated argument. They immediately stopped yelling when they saw Booger and Rose walking down the pathway.

"What do you think that was about?" Rose asked her husband.

"I don't know. My hearing isn't as good as it used to be, but I thought I heard Diane's name mentioned just before they stopped talking.

The rain had stopped. The clouds gave way to mostly sunny skies, and a large rainbow could be seen in the distance as the couple got in Booger's vintage Corvette.

As her husband started to roll the top down, Rose grabbed his arm. "Let's leave the top up this time," Rose said with a smile.

"OK, dear."

It was a short drive to Mike Robinson's office. He was on the second floor of a two-story brick building that looked like it was constructed in the '40s or '50s.

Booger pulled into a small lot adjacent to the building.

"Are you excited, Rose?" Booger asked.

"No, but I am nervous. Why would Diane leave the bulk of her estate to me? We were just friends."

"I don't know, but I guess we'll find out soon."

The couple walked into the building and then took the elevator to the second floor, Suite 202.

Booger opened the door for his wife to see a small waiting room with a receptionist behind a desk, and Ida seated in a chair just to the right of the door.

"Hello," Rose responded.

"Hello," Ida responded in a low tone that was barely audible.

"Are you the only one here?" Booger asked.

"Well, my brothers will be here shortly."

"You must be Rose McClain?" the receptionist asked.

"Yes, that's me, and this is my husband," she responded, gesturing toward Booger.

"Wonderful, just take a seat, and once everyone has arrived, I'll let Mr. Robinson know."

Rose sat down and looked at Ida, hoping to strike up a casual conversation, but Ida was staring directly at the floor with body language that clearly showed she wasn't in the mood for conversation.

At 2 pm precisely, the office door opened, and in walked Brandon and Cornilus Landers. Brandon didn't say a word. He simply walked to his sister and took a chair next to her. Cornilus, a distinguished-looking gentleman wearing a tailored blue pinstriped suit, walked over to Booger and held out his hand. "Nice to finally meet you, Mr. McClain. I've heard a lot about you."

"And you, too, Mr. Landers."

Then he turned his attention to Rose. "And you must be Rose?"

"Yes. And you must be Cornilus."

"Yes, ma'am."

The awkwardness was broken when the receptionist announced to the attorney that all parties were present.

"Send them in, Ms. Perl."

The receptionist motioned to the group and escorted them down a short hallway to an office.

Before opening the door, she asked, "Can I get anyone refreshments? We have bottled water and coffee."

"I'll take a cup of coffee," Booger said. "Black."

Everyone else nodded their heads 'no'.

Then, the receptionist opened the office door, and the attorney stood up from his large maple desk to greet everyone. Mike Robinson was dressed in business casual, wearing a light blue dress shirt and dark blue slacks, no tie, and no sports coat. He was a young man, no more than thirty, Booger figured, with thick black wavy hair and a rather large, round face on a thin-framed body.

He introduced himself, shook hands with everyone, and pointed to five chairs sitting in front of his desk. "Please sit down."

Mike Robinson sat down, put a pair of reading glasses on, and shuffled several papers on his desk as Ms. Perl returned with a cup of steaming hot black coffee and paced in front of Booger.

He took a sip and whispered to his wife, "It's not Folgers."

She jabbed him in the side, causing him to spill a couple of drops on his blue jeans. He wiped them with a napkin as everyone watched, except for the attorney, who was still shuffling papers.

Then, Attorney Robinson broke the silence when he cleared his throat and began to talk.

"I have in front of me, gentlemen and ladies, Ms. Diane Landers' last Will and Testament, which she signed in my presence and the presence of a notary one week ago today."

He cleared his throat again before reading from the Will.

To my only living relatives, Cornilus, Brandon, and Ida Landers, who refused to take me in after my parents passed away, forcing me to grow up in an orphanage, and to the same relatives whose greed led them to steal from the business my father owned, I leave nothing but my empathy toward your shallow, uncaring and loveless lives.

To my best and only friend, Rose McClain, who asked nothing of me but gave her heart and friendship when I needed it most, I leave my entire estate, including the Landers Theatre.

To that, Cornilus stood up and exclaimed, "I'll contest that will. My niece was coerced into signing it. Mrs. McClain, prepare for a long, legal battle before you see a dime from my dear niece's estate."

Then Cornilus stormed out of the attorney's office, his brother and sister following behind.

"Ha, well, that went well," Booger said, trying to add a little levity to the situation.

Rose sat motionless, her mouth partially open and her eyes fixated on the wall directly in front of her. She was in shock and sat frozen for a few seconds before talking.

"Mr. Robinson, what does that all mean?"

"It means, young lady, that you have suddenly become a millionaire."

"Really?" she asked in disbelief.

"Yes. With cash and the current value of stocks and bonds and considering the fair market price of the Landers Theatre, I'd estimate your inherited estate to be worth somewhere in the vicinity of four million dollars."

"Oh my," Rose exclaimed, still in shock.

"Mr. Robinson," Booger asked, "What are the chances of the Landers children getting a judge to revoke the will?"

"Slim to none, I'd say. That will was drawn up properly and in the presence of witnesses. Ms. Landers, I might add, was in control of all her faculties and was under no duress when she signed the will. She knew exactly what she was doing, and I'll testify to that in a court of law if need be."

"Thanks, Mr. Robinson. Is that all? Can we leave now?"

"Well, yes. But first, here is a briefcase with keys to Ms. Landers' safety deposit box that will contain her stocks and bonds, other important documents, and her bank account information. It also contains keys to the Landers Theatre, and given Cornilus Landers' reaction, may I suggest you change the locks? I'll be in touch with you in a few days to iron out any other details of Ms. Landers' estate."

The couple shook hands with Mr. Robinson, grabbed the briefcase, and left.

Rose didn't say a word on the walk to the car. She got in the Corvette, buckled up, and just smiled.

"Well, how's it feel to be a millionaire, sweetheart?"

"About the same as it did to be a thousandaire."

"Mind if I roll the top down, Rose?"

"No, I could use some air."

"Hey, all that talk about money really worked up an appetite for me. Do you mind if I go through the McDonalds drive-thru and get a quarter-pounder with cheese value meal?"

"Fine. And Booger, why don't you make it a double quarter pounder with cheese, and I'll even pay for it."

CHAPTER ELEVEN
THE NEW MILLIONAIRE

"Money, money, money, money – mon-ey," Rose sang in the shower as she thought about how her fortunes had changed. She knew that this newfound wealth came with strings attached, but she couldn't help but feel like a bubbly little girl.

"Hello, yes, I am Rose McClain, owner of the Landers Theatre," she mouthed to herself in the foggy bathroom mirror after she showered. "Yes, darling, I am prepared to discuss the fine arts with you."

Rose had been closer to being poor than she was to being rich her entire life. She had learned to enjoy the simple pleasures of life, and she was determined that her new wealth would not change her one bit. Although Rose would be the first to admit that money can have a way of lessening life's little burdens.

Booger had been the one to pay the bills and to take on the responsibility of the main breadwinner. He had been generous to Rose and had given her everything she wanted, but now she didn't need to depend on her husband financially anymore. She had a newfound independence, and it felt damn good to her.

Her biggest concern right now was the Landers Theatre. She just didn't have the time or energy to manage it. It was a responsibility that she didn't want. But, on the other hand, it had been in Diane Landers' family for quite some time, and Diane wanted to make the theatre more successful than it was. Diane had left the theatre to her, and Rose felt she needed to make sure the business was running the way her friend would have wanted.

Rose also knew that Diane suspected the other Landers' kids were skimming money from the Theatre, which presented quite a quandary for her. On the one hand, it would be easiest to leave the management of the theatre to Cornilus, Brandon, and Ida. On the other hand, Rose had no guarantee that they wouldn't continue stealing from the theatre's coffers, eventually destroying the success of the theatre.

In Rose's mind, there was only one thing she could do to protect her friend's legacy. And that was a decision that would not be received well by the Landers family.

"Booger, we need to go back to the inn so I can talk to Brandon and Ida."

"Do you want me to be with you?"

"No, honey, I think this is something I need to do by myself."

When they arrived, Randolph greeted them at the front desk. "Hello, Mr. and Mrs. McClain. How is your stay at the Walnut Street Inn so far?"

"Fine," Booger responded. "Except for the ghosts that moved in next door. They kept me up most of the night."

Randolph laughed. Booger did not.

"Randolph?" Rose asked. "Do you know where Brandon and Ida are?"

"I believe they are on the back patio talking to Mr. Baczenas. Cornilus Landers is with them, too."

"OK, thanks."

"Rose, are you sure that you don't want me to go with you?"

"Yes, I'm sure."

"OK. I'll just wait in the bar. If you need me, I'll just be a shout away."

"Thanks, sweetie."

As Rose headed for the back sliding glass door leading to the patio, Booger saw Pat sitting at the bar and decided to take a seat next to him.

Randolph pulled double duty as the person behind the front desk and the bartender rushed over to take Booger's order.

"Mr. McClain, what can I get you to drink?"

"I believe I'll have a Buffalo Trace Bourbon. Make it a double with one ice cube."

"Certainly."

"Mr. Williams, do you want me to get you another whiskey?"

"Yes, thank you, Randolph, and please call me Pat."

"Yes, sir."

"Pat, what have you and your wife been up to since arriving in Springfield?" Booger asked.

"Nothing, really. My wife, Sue, hasn't felt good since breakfast, so she's up in the room resting. I've been exploring the grounds. I was hoping to play a round of golf today with my brother, but he seems a little preoccupied and, I believe, a little stressed, too."

"Why do you think he's stressed?"

"I don't know. It could be my imagination, but I have a gut feeling that it has something to do with the Landers. He got into an argument with Brandon earlier today, and now he's meeting with all three of the Landers, including the big brother, Cornilus. My brother wasn't smiling when they asked to meet with him. Quite frankly, Booger, I think my brother may be in some sort of trouble."

"What kind of trouble?"

"I wish I knew. But he's just not his normal self this weekend. He even tried to talk me and Sue out of coming down to visit, even though we had planned this trip for over a month. Bob had even set up a tee time for us for today and tomorrow. But now, we've already missed today's tee time."

Just then, Rose returned to the bar area.

"Well, that was a quick talk," Booger said. "Randolph hasn't even finished mixing our drinks yet."

"I didn't meet with them. There's something weird going on, Booger. When I got close to the door, I could hear shouting going on. Then I saw Cornilus screaming at Bob with his finger right up to his face. Ida was crying, and Brandon was consoling her. It did not look like a conversation that I wanted to interrupt."

Randolph set the drinks down in front of Pat and Booger, and then he turned to Rose. "Can I get you something to drink, Mrs. McClain?"

"I'll have whatever my husband is having."

"Sweetie, I'm having a double bourbon, and you don't like bourbon."

"That's fine. I need something strong."

"Randolph, what's in the basement?" Rose asked.

"Not much, really. Seasonal decorations mostly."

"Rose, why are you interested in what's in the basement?"

"Just something I heard Cornilus say when he was yelling at Bob."

"What?"

"He told him that he damn well better keep that basement door locked if he knows what's good for him."

"Interesting," Booger replied, taking a sip of bourbon.

"That wasn't the thing I heard him say that bothered me

the most, Booger."

"What was it?"

"Cornilus tuned to Brandon and told him that he better keep Ida quiet, or both of them could end up down in the basement like the others."

"Shit. I think I need to take a look in the basement."

"Randolf?" Booger asked. "Do you have any rooms available here in the Inn?"

"No, I believe they are all being renovated. Except for the one room on the third floor. But I don't think you'd want that one."

"Why?"

"Well, it was the attic until a few years ago when Mr. Williams converted it to an extra bedroom. It's drafty up there, and there aren't any windows. Besides…"

"Besides what, Randolph?"

"Well, sir, there was a suicide committed in that room, a hanging. A man named Stevenson from one of those East Coast tabloids. He came to town to do an article about ghosts haunting the inn. At the time, renovations of that room had just been completed. And all other rooms were occupied that weekend. So, Mr. Williams offered it to Mr. Stevenson. The next morning, Mr. Stevenson didn't come down for breakfast. Mrs. Williams rang his room several times. But there was no answer. Finally, Mr. Williams went up to check on him. That's when he found him hanging from the ceiling fan by his own belt. We haven't had guests stay in that room since."

"Oh, my," Rose gasped.

"Randolph, if we could, I'd like Rose and me to stay in that room."

"What?" Rose exclaimed, giving her husband a nasty look.

"Well, I'll need to ask Mr. Williams first."

"Fine, just let us know when we can move over, the sooner the better."

"Yes, sir."

Pat, listening intently to the conversation, asked, "Mr. McClain, are you sure that you want to stay in that room? The idea of someone dying in that room would unnerve me."

"Nah. It doesn't bother me."

"Well, it bothers me, old man," Rose said with a concerned look.

"You know, I don't know what's worse," Pat Added. "Knowing that someone died in that room or the idea that their ghost may still occupy it."

"Oh, that makes me feel much better," Rose said in a sarcastic tone.

"To change the subject, Mr. McClain, do you think my brother is in trouble?"

"I don't know, Mr. Williams."

"If he is, can you help him?"

"That's what I want to do, but please keep anything you overhear today to yourself."

"Oh, I will."

"Don't even tell your wife. After all, there is no sense involving her."

"I understand."

A few minutes later, Cornilus Landers stormed out of the inn. He didn't even notice Booger and Rose seated at the bar. Behind him walked Brandon and Ida. Brandon was helping his sister, who was wiping tears from her eyes. Brandon glanced over at the bar and, without saying anything, continued walking his sister up the stairs.

Bob walked in soon after with a concerned look on his face. Seeing the others at the bar, he showed a forced smile and walked into the bar to greet his guests.

"Hello, Booger and Rose. I trust you've had a good day."

"Yes," Rose responded.

"Good. Good. And, brother, how are you doing this afternoon?"

"Fine, thanks. However, I think we've missed our tee time."

"Oh, my goodness, I completely forgot. Let's plan on tomorrow, little brother."

"Bob, where is your lovely wife? I haven't seen her since breakfast," Rose said.

"Her mother took sick, and my wife drove to Kansas City to spend a few days with her."

"Oh my, that was rather sudden," Rose said, glancing over at Booger.

"Yes. It was." Bob responded.

"Bob, can I ask you something?"

"Sure, Booger, what is it?"

"Rose and I feel a little lonely over at the Carriage House by ourselves. Would it be possible for us to get a room here? Pat mentioned that there is a room on the third floor that's not undergoing renovations. Do you suppose we could move to that room?"

Bob shot a glance at his brother. It was an unhappy look.

"Yes, I think that can be arranged. However, that room hasn't been occupied in some time. We'll need to clean it and change the bed sheets and towels. Perhaps we could move you and your wife over tomorrow morning."

"Yes, that would be great."

After Bob left, Booger turned to Randolph and said, "Thanks for thinking of that room, Randolph. I'm sure Rose and I will be much happier staying in the inn, close to the others."

"Speak for yourself, old man," Rose said.

"It will be fine, Rose. I'm sure what happened to that last guest had nothing to do with that room."

"Just like you were sure it wasn't going to rain?"

Booger didn't answer.

Randolph showed a nervous smile and walked away.

That evening, at least the early portion of it, was largely uneventful. Booger took his wife out to Red Lobster, then came back to the inn for a nightcap and returned to their room at the Carriage House. Much of the evening was spent reassuring Rose that there were no ghosts and that soon he would find out who and why someone was trying to frighten them away from the bed and breakfast."

Rose believed what her husband was saying was true. It just didn't make sense that there were actually ghosts haunting the Walnut Street Inn. It had to be someone or some people trying to frighten them away from the establishment. But who and why? Neither Rose nor Booger had the answers.

However, the detective had a plan. At a little past midnight, Booger and Rose stepped out of room 213 and walked next door to room 215. Booger put his ear against the door and listened for any sounds coming from inside the room. Confident that no one was inside, the detective used his flat metal tool, which he called 'man's best friend,' to unlock the door. Both detectives walked inside. When they turned on the lights, it was as if they had gone back a century in time.

Colonial-style furniture, floral wallpaper, a dresser with a dainty, upholstered stool, and a white oak poster bed. Next to the bed on a nightstand was a 1920s-style phone with a rotary dial. Against one wall was an old phonograph. Covering the wood floor was a large, hand-hooked wool rug with red and ivory floral patterns.

"Old man, this room is spooky. If I believed in ghosts, this is the room that I would imagine them haunting."

Booger ran his hand over the dresser and the nightstand, then he examined the bedspread. "You know this room is incredibly clean, no dust, and the bed sheets appear to be fresh, probably changed recently.

"Maybe the ghosts like a clean room."

"More likely, someone's been in here recently to do a thorough cleaning."

"Yeah, ghosts."

Booger went over every square inch of that room.

"What are you doing?"

"If I'm right, there has to be another way to get into this room besides coming through the front door."

"OK, how can I help?" Rose asked.

"You search the right side of the room, and I'll search the left."

"What am I looking for?"

"A hatch in the floor, a secret door. You'll know when you find it, Rose."

Inch by inch, the couple searched that room. They moved the bed and looked underneath. They moved the carpet and all the furniture to search underneath and behind. The bathroom was the last place they searched. Behind a large mirror extending from the floor almost to the ceiling, Rose noticed something odd.

"Booger, come here. Do you see a slight crease in the wallpaper behind this mirror?"

"No."

"Trust me, it's there."

Rose pressed her fingertips against the crease and then pulled. A hidden door in the wall opened, revealing a wooden staircase going down.

"Sweetie, you're amazing. I would have never spotted that."

"I know. You have a difficult time seeing your underwear laying on the bathroom floor."

"I spot it. I'm just not in a rush to move it. You never know when you'll need spare underwear in the bathroom."

Booger looked on the wall of the stairs for a light switch. Not finding one, he grabbed his flashlight and started down the stairs. "Stay here, Rose. I'll be back soon."

"No way, old man. I'm coming with you."

Booger knew it was futile to argue with his wife, so he started down the stairs with Rose right behind him.

The stairs, old and creaky, went down about twenty feet and opened in a dark basement.

"I didn't know there was a basement in the Carriage House," Rose said.

"Me either," Booger replied.

There were no lights down there. The ceiling was barely six feet high, held up by large wood planks like what you would see in a cave. The basement had cinder block walls and a dirt floor and was approximately six feet wide by six feet deep. It was completely empty.

Little creatures of the night, mainly water bugs and field mice, scurried across the floor. Rose, not fond of them, kept her eyes peeled to the walls.

"Booger, shine your light over there," she said, pointing to the wall on her right side.

When he did, both noticed a hole in the wall. As they got closer, they saw it was more than a hole. It was a tunnel barely large enough for Booger's large frame to crawl into.

"Are you coming, Rose?"

"Damn right, I am."

The two crawled in darkness with only the narrow beam of light from Booger's flashlight to guide the way.

They had traveled only about twenty feet when they encountered a new wall. Booger pushed, and a hidden door opened up to a much larger tunnel, one where both detectives could stand inside.

The tunnel veered to the left and to the right. Booger chose to go left. "I think this way leads us toward the inn."

A few feet down the tunnel was a steel door on the right side. Inside, he could hear faint cries. He turned the knob on the door, but it was bolted locked. "Man's best friend is not enough for this one," he said aloud. Unable to open it to see inside, the detective chose to move on.

"It sounds like people in pain inside that room," Rose said to her husband.

"Yes, I'll need to come back another time when I have the tools to open the door."

Down the tunnel, about ten feet, Booger and Rose heard voices and footsteps coming. So, they chose to go back to the opening, into the smaller tunnel, and back to the Carriage. They moved quickly and quietly so as not to be seen or heard by whoever was coming.

Back in room 215, they shut the hidden door and put the mirror back in place.

"Let's get back to our room, Rose. I don't want whoever is

coming to discover us in this room."

Ten minutes after getting back to room 213, weird noises began coming from the room next door. Doors shut and opened loudly. The phonograph played Louis Armstrong and roaring twenties jazz loudly.

The noise went on for about thirty minutes and then went silent.

"I guess the ghosts have retired for the evening," Rose said.

"More likely, the Landers siblings have retired for the evening," Booger remarked.

"You think it's the Landers kids pretending to be ghosts?"

"I don't know," Booger replied. "But if I were a betting man, I would say it was the Landers' siblings or some of their cronies."

CHAPTER TWELVE
THE BASEMENT

The next morning, at breakfast, only Bob and Pat were present. "Where's your better half, Pat?" Booger asked.

"Sue's still sick in bed. I'll take an orange juice up to her when I go back."

"What about Brandon and Ida? Aren't they coming down for breakfast?"

"I haven't seen them. I don't think they slept in their room last night," Bob answered.

"By the way, Booger, your room upstairs is ready." Bob handed the McClains a key to room 313. "You can move at any time. I'm afraid, though, that the room is not as nice as the one at the Carriage House." Bob said.

So, after dining on canned fruit, stale donuts, and boxed cereal, the detectives went back to their room at the Carriage House, packed, and moved over to the main house. To say that their new room at the inn was not as nice as the one at the Carriage House was an understatement. There were no windows. The ceiling was of different sizes, maybe four feet tall where the bed was, and then seven feet tall on the other side of the room. It was obvious the room had once been an attic. It was cold and damp, with poor lighting.

After napping for a couple of hours, a luxury neither really had with the office to run, Booger awoke and announced to his wife, still trying to rub the sleep out of her eyes, "Rose, I think you deserve to be taken out for a night on the town."

"Whose taking me?"

"Funny, Rose."

"What do you say I take you out to an early dinner to celebrate your recent entry into the Millionaires' Club. Let's go someplace special for dinner tonight, Rose, someplace worthy of your new lot in life."

"In Springfield?"

"Yes, we have plenty of fine restaurants in Springfield."

"Someplace special that you can wear blue jeans, a sports shirt, and cowboy boots, too?"

"Yeah, someplace real classy but also casual."

"Uh-huh."

"I'm thinking Black Sheep Burgers."

"Classy?"

"Yeah, they let every class of people in there."

"You know, Booger, normally, I would give you trouble over selecting a burger place to take your wife on a special date, but the fact is, I'm in the mood for a good burger."

"Can we stop by Andy's Frozen Custard on the way back?"

"Your wish is my command, darling."

"Uh-huh."

The downtown location of Black Sheep Burgers was only ten minutes away. They did not take reservations, and Booger anticipated a crowd, so the couple left the inn fifteen minutes before 5 pm.

The parking lot was nearly empty, and the restaurant was the same.

"We must of beat the crowd here, Rose."

"Uh-huh."

The couple took a seat near the bar area. Just as they sat down, a server named Roxy came over and handed the couple menus. "Can I get you something to drink?"

"Roxy, this is my lovely wife, Rose, and I'm Booger. This is a very special date for us. It's our 27th monthly anniversary."

"Almost 33rd monthly anniversary," Rose interrupted.

"Really?" Booger asked.

"Really."

"OK. Well, Roxie, it's almost our 33rd monthly anniversary, and we'd like a special beer, something exotic, something not from around here."

"We have Bud Light."

"Sounds perfect, dear," Rose responded. "Make it two of them."

"Do you have them in a bottle?" Booger asked.

"Is there any other way?" Roxie said with a smile.

A few minutes later, she returned with two ice-cold bottles of Bud Light. "Have you decided on dinner yet?"

"Yes, Rose, you go first."

"I'm going to take the 'Don't Go Bacon My Heart Burger,' well done."

Booger looked at the menu one more time before ordering, "I'll take the 'Ugly Cheeseburger' medium rare, and we'll take two orders of the Apple n' Hickory Smoked fries, and why don't you bring us some of those habanero cheese curds, too."

"You got it," Roxie responded as she walked away.

After taking a sip of beer, Booger turned to Rose. "When are you going to talk to the Landers' kids about getting out of the theatre?"

"As soon as I see them again."

"You know they're not going to take the news well."

"Yes, I know."

"I really think we should talk to them together," Booger said, putting his arm on Rose's shoulder.

"No, it's my decision and something I think I need to do alone."

"Rose, you know there's a possibility that your friend Diane gave them the same bad news right before she fell down those stairs."

"Yes, I know. But I'm not going to talk to them late at night in that Theatre, and besides, I've got a stun gun and a 38-caliber pistol in my handbag."

"Even so, I want to be close by when you meet with them."

"Booger, what do you think is going on at the inn?"

"What do you mean?"

"You know. In the basement."

"I don't know, Rose. It's weird, but we are on the case, and we will find out."

"When?"

"Tonight, after everyone has gone to bed."

"The door's locked. How are you going to get the key?"

"Well, if it's not around the front desk, I'll just have to break in."

"Won't that make noise?"

"Nah. I've got a special tool that can open almost any lock."

"Almost?"

"Almost."

"That's comforting."

The conversation was interrupted when Roxy appeared carrying two plates of burgers, fries, and cheese curds.

"That smells good," Booger commented. "Looks good,

too. Can we get two more ice-cold Bud Lights, too, Roxy?"

"Absolutely."

For the next ten minutes, not a word was uttered as Booger chowed down on his burger, only coming up for air to wash it down with a sip of his cold Bud Light. He had finished his burger, all the fries, and half of the cheese curds before Rose had finished half of her burger.

"What's the matter? Aren't you hungry, dear?"

"No, not really. I keep thinking about what might be going on at the bed and breakfast. You know, I think Bob and Cindy are in trouble."

"Rose, if you're not going to finish that burger, can I have the rest of it?"

She handed him her plate, and Booger took the remainder of the burger.

"There's something fishy going on there. That argument on the patio with Cornilus was ugly, and didn't you find it suspicious that his wife suddenly left town supposedly because her mother was ill?"

"You going to eat those fries, sweetie?"

"And what Cornilus said about the basement has got to make you wonder what is down there and how involved Bob and Cindy might be."

"Can you pass me your smoked fries, darling?"

Rose passed the plate over to Booger. He grabbed a handful, stuffed them in his mouth, and slid the rest of them onto his plate.

"And did you see how all three of them completely ignored us and stormed out of the inn?"

"What about those cheese curds? Are you going to finish them?"

"You know that we haven't seen Brandon or Ida since they left with their brother. Where do you suppose they went?"

Booger downed the remainder of his beer and said, "Sweetie, are you going to finish that beer?"

Rose nodded, and Booger grabbed it.

"I'm also worried about Sue. Her husband said she got sick not long after breakfast. She looked and acted fine to me that morning. You don't suppose she got some sort of food poisoning, do you? Although that doesn't make sense because no one else got sick."

"Rose, do they have dessert here?"

A few minutes later, Booger paid the bill, left a generous tip for Roxy, and the couple got in the red Corvette and drove to the nearest Andy's Frozen Custard.

"A large Booty Daddy concrete with extra fudge for me, and my wife will take a large James Brownie Funky Jackhammer with extra hot fudge."

"Booger, make it small. I'm not that hungry."

"Sweetie, if you don't finish it, I will. I'm starving."

As Booger's red Corvette turned the corner on Walnut Street, they saw the ambulance pull up in front of the inn. Booger pulled up a few feet behind the ambulance just as he saw Cindy Williams being wheeled out on a stretcher. Pat was walking beside the stretcher, holding her hand. Bob was standing on the front porch.

"What happened, Bob?" Rose asked.

"They think it might be the flu or something like it. The doctor wanted to admit her, get some fluids in her, and keep an eye on her for a day or two. Pat's going to stay with her, at least for tonight."

"Oh my."

After the ambulance left, Rose and Booger walked inside the inn. That's when they saw Ida and Brandon sitting alone at a table in the bar.

"Well, I guess they are back. Odd that they didn't go outside to see what was going on with Cindy," Rose commented.

"Yeah, but look at it this way – this gives you a good opportunity to talk to Brandon and Ida.

I'll sit at the bar with Randolf so you can talk to them alone and have me close enough in case the conversation goes south."

"OK."

Booger sat at the bar and said to the bartender, "Randolph, good man, I'll take a double Buffalo Trace bourbon with one ice cube."

"Sorry, Mr. McClain, the Buffalo Trace is gone. You finished it off last night."

"Damn, what other whiskey do you have?"

"The only other one we have is our house whiskey, Wood Hat Blue Corn Whiskey."

"Triple distilled and aged for an entire year, right?"

"Well, aged for part of a year anyway."

"OK, give me a double with three ice cubes and some soda water to dilute its flavor. And better give me some Tabasco sauce that I can pour over my tongue to numb my sense of taste before I take a drink."

As Rose approached the table where Brandon and Ida were sitting, their conversation stopped. "What can we do for you, Mrs. McClain?" Brandon asked.

"I just need a couple of minutes of your time."

"OK. Sit down."

Rose took a seat across from Brandon and next to Ida. Ida said nothing and looked directly at her brother.

"I know it must have been a shock yesterday in Mike Robinson's office."

"That's an understatement, Mrs. McClain."

"Yes, well, it came as a surprise to me, too. Diane had never mentioned putting me in her will."

"Regardless, she apparently did, Mrs. McClain, and as a result, Cornilus, my sister, and I are pretty much left out in the cold."

"Yes, I certainly understand. But now, as owner of the Landers Theatre, I've got some difficult decisions to make."

"I don't know, Mrs. McClain," Brandon said in a tone that sounded a bit sarcastic, "It seems that you could simply give us the Landers Theatre and let the family run it. You obviously are going to be very wealthy as a result of Diane's estate. You don't really need the theatre."

"No, you're right. I don't, and quite frankly, I don't know anything about running a theatre, nor do I feel that I have the time or energy for such an endeavor."

"So, you're considering giving us the Landers Theatre?"

"No, but I am considering selling it."

"OK, Mrs. McClain, cut to the chase. How much money do you want for it?"

"I'm not sure. I don't even know the value of the theatre. But I intend to find out. I plan to hire an outside company to check the books and evaluate the current value of the Landers Theatre. Once I'm sure of its value, I'll put it on the market."

"Do you really think that's what Diane Landers would have wanted?"

"No. I think my friend would have wanted to see the theatre thrive, to become as successful as possible, and to leave a legacy for her family."

"Then let her family buy the theatre from you. I assure you we'll give you a fair price."

"Mr. Landers, when I spoke of Diane's family, I wasn't thinking of you or your siblings. I was thinking of Diane's parents and her little brother. From what Diane told me, your family pretty much abandoned her after her family died."

"Now, wait a second…"

"No, you need to hear this, Mr. Landers, and you, too, Ida. Diane was put in an orphanage because no one in your family would take her in, and as for your operation of the theatre, she suspected you and your siblings were skimming from it. She had even hired a CPA firm to examine the books the day after her fatal accident, if it was an accident. I intend to sell the theatre to someone who will take care of it, someone who will help it grow and thrive, just like Diane would have wanted. And there is no way on God's green earth that I would let your family get its hands on it."

"We'll just see about that, Mrs. McClain. If you want a fight, you've come to the wrong family," Brandon said just before storming off. Ida, who hadn't said a word, followed her brother out the front door.

Booger walked over, put his arm around his wife, and said, "That seemed to go well."

"It did. Didn't it?" Rose said, trying to force a smile.

"So, what are you going to do until you find a buyer?"

"I guess I'll run it myself. I'm sure there are people who can help me until I find someone to take over."

"Well, I don't think you can count on the Landers' siblings to help."

"No."

That night was extremely quiet in the inn. Sue Williams

was in the hospital. Her husband was staying with her. Brandon and Ida Landers did not come back after storming off. Randolf took the night off. That left Bob as the only other person in the inn that night. Booger figured that made it the perfect time to take a look at what was in the basement. The detective thought he'd sneak down in the wee hours of the morning when he was certain Bob was asleep.

As it turned out, he didn't need to wait that long. The office phone rang at about 10 pm that night. Bob answered and soon after rushed out of the inn, leaving the McClains completely alone in the bed and breakfast.

When Booger heard the front door shut, he kissed his wife and told her to stay in the room and to call him on his cell phone if anyone came in the front door. Booger set his phone on vibrate and headed downstairs.

The lights were off in the lobby and bar area. Booger checked the front door. It was locked, too. A bell hung on the inside of the door, which would alert Rose if someone were to enter the building.

The detective moved quickly to the basement door. It was locked, but it was a simple lock that his best friend had no problem overcoming. The basement, really more of a cellar than a basement, was completely dark. There were no windows to shine in the moonlight and streetlights from outside. Booger blindly reached his hands around both sides of the wall, searching for a light switch. When he finally found it, he flipped the switch, but no light came on. Luckily, he had brought a small flashlight with him. He turned it on, and it shone a narrow light down the stairs to the cellar floor. Booger shut the basement door behind him and slowly walked down the creaky wooden stairs - eight narrow stairs with a steep incline.

After two steps onto the dirt floor of the cellar, he felt something crawl up one of his pant legs. Then something bit him, not hard, but enough of a bite to make him jump just a little. He immediately shined the flashlight downward on his leg. That's when he saw one large mouse coming out of his pants and scurrying away. About a dozen of the mouse's buddies were on the floor immediately in front of Booger. He hollered, and they all ran to the back wall and disappeared.

Booger shook off his nerves and steadied the flashlight straight ahead. It was damp and cold in that cellar. Ceiling beams were only about six feet from the ground, forcing the detective to bend over as he walked. Spider webs dangled from the ceiling. The place was infested with rodents. Shelves straight ahead contained assorted boxes and holiday decorations. In one corner was an old, loud furnace and two large water heaters.

As he stepped closer to one wall, he heard the sound. Someone, something large, was moving around to the right of him. He quickly moved the flashlight, and the beam of light spotted something large, standing up and moving quickly. Then the flashlight went dark. *"Damn batteries,"* Booger whispered under his breath.

Now, he was blinded by the dark. Booger couldn't see more than a few inches in front of him, but he could hear something moving toward him. He stood frozen in place, shaking the flashlight, hoping for it to turn back on, hoping for just a few more seconds of light.

Suddenly, he heard something directly behind him. Before he could turn around, he heard a cracking sound from the back of his head. He heard the sound before he felt the pain. Then he collapsed to the ground and passed out.

CHAPTER THIRTEEN
MURDER AT THE INN

"Wake up, Booger, wake up," were the first words he heard as he started to come to.

"Stop shaking me, Rose. I'm awake. Just give me a few seconds. My head is pounding. Why'd you come down here? I told you to stay in the room."

"Booger, I heard a door open, and I tried to call you, but there wasn't any answer. Then I heard noises coming from the second floor. I ran downstairs and saw the basement door open, so I came down looking for you. You scared me to death, old man. What happened?"

"I'm not exactly sure. I think someone snuck up behind me and clobbered me over the head with something."

"It might be this pipe lying next to you."

"You think?"

"Booger, I think someone is still here. I haven't heard the bell go off at the front door, but I heard a loud sound from upstairs about five minutes ago."

The detective slowly stood up and steadied himself. The back of his head was coated with dried blood. After taking a few slow steps and determining he was steady enough to walk, Booger pulled a gun from his shoulder harness and started up the basement stairs with Rose right behind him.

The lobby was dark. Booger had left his flashlight in the

cellar in his hurry to get upstairs. Every step he took seemed to echo in the darkness. His line of sight was only inches from his face as he worked his way closer to the stairs leading to the second floor. Then he stopped. *"Light from the outside would provide him a little more visibility,"* he thought. So he changed directions and moved to the front door. It was locked and deadbolted from the inside. Booger unlocked it and opened the door. Coming up the steps leading to the wooden front porch were Detective Walter Jelks and two police officers. Two patrol cars were parked on the street in front of the inn with lights flashing.

"Detective, what are you doing here?" Booger asked, surprised to see the police.

"Getting ready to leave, Mr. and Mrs. McClain?" the detective asked while ignoring Booger's question.

"No detective. Just trying to let some light into the place. It seems that the power is out."

Two more police cars, lights flashing, pulled up outside.

"What's going on, detective?" Booger asked.

Walter Jelks ignored him and rushed up the stairs to the third floor. Two officers trailed him, and Booger and Rose followed.

At the top of the stairs, the detective moved down the hallway to Room 313. There, he stopped and unholstered his gun. Pointing directly ahead, he knocked on the door and hollered, "Police, open the door."

"That's our room, Jelks. What's going on?"

Jelks didn't answer.

The door to room 313 was partially open, so when no one answered, Jelks pushed the door open and walked inside, gun pointed straight ahead.

"Police. Drop your weapon and come out," he ordered.

There was no response. Walker Jelks moved forward slowly, pivoting his gun from side to side as the other two policemen, guns drawn, also covered him.

The room looked empty. The bed was unmade, but no one was there. But there were two areas to check. The closet door was closed, and the bathroom door was partially open. The detective checked the closet first. Clothes were hung up, and two suitcases, one empty and one partially empty, lay on the floor. Otherwise, the space was empty.

Then the detective moved to the bathroom, where he pushed open the door. There on the floor, fully dressed, with a bullet hole in his head and blood puddled on the floor, was Bob Williams.

Rose gasped when she saw the body.

"You need to leave right now," Walter Jelks ordered Booger and Rose. "This is a crime scene."

"This is our room, detective," Booger said.

"Stay downstairs, and don't leave. I'll need to talk to both of you later."

"Sargent," the detective said, looking at the policeman directly behind him, "Take Mr. and Mrs. McClain downstairs and stay with them until I have a chance to talk to them."

Walter Jelks called the homicide in, sealed off the room, and waited for the CSI people to arrive. Soon, there was a flurry of police activity both outside and inside the inn. The coroner soon arrived, as did a CSI team. Yellow police tape covered the entrance to the room as well as the area outside the inn. Police prevented onlookers from getting on the grounds of the Bed and Breakfast.

Inside room 313, a small caliber handgun lay next to the body. Blood was not found in any other part of the room. It was on the victim and had pooled underneath him. There was no evidence that the body had been moved. The room door had not been jimmied or forced open. Either someone opened it from the inside or had a key to open it from the outside.

Two women's size small black gloves were found lying on the floor of the closet underneath one of the suitcases.

But the most damning evidence was a note that had been wadded up and left in the trash can next to the desk. The note simply read, "I have evidence of a second will leaving everything to the Landers siblings." It was signed "B."

The CSI team dusted fingerprints on the note, the inside of the gloves, and the handgun, as well as on the victim. They would also send away to test for gun residue on the gloves.

The sun had been up for several hours by the time investigators finished in room 313.

Booger and Rose were waiting in the bar area when the detective came downstairs.

"Mr. and Mrs. McClain, please explain to me everything you did between midnight and 6 am this morning."

Booger took the lead and explained to the detective about the argument his wife had overheard on the patio between Bob and the Landers siblings, including the comment about the basement. Because of his suspicions about what might be going on in the basement, Booger decided to investigate it after everyone went to sleep that night. As it turned out, Bob left the inn that evening, and no one else was present, so he waited a bit and then walked down to the basement door. He asked Rose to call his cell phone if she heard anyone coming through the front door. He then explained that while searching around in the dark, someone hit him over the head from behind, and he passed out. The next thing he knew, Rose was trying to shake him awake. He and Rose had just come up from the basement when Walker Jelks and two policemen arrived.

Rose then confirmed what her husband had said, telling the same story and talking about the argument she had heard between Cornilus Landers and Bob Williams. "Cornilus seemed concerned that the basement door had been left unlocked and that there were things down there that he didn't want others to see. He seemed to threaten Bob by saying that he could end up like others that were in that basement."

Rose told the detective that she heard doors open and close and heard voices. It was then that she called Booger's cell phone, but there was no answer. Then she heard someone on the second floor. They seemed to go into one of the rooms, and when she heard the door shut, she quickly and quietly left her room and went downstairs and into the basement, where she found Booger lying on the floor. "That's about all there is, detective. After Booger awoke, we went upstairs, and you were outside the front door.

"Was the door locked or unlocked?"

"Locked detective from the inside, both deadbolted and locked."

"What about your room? Did you leave it partially open in your rush to get downstairs?"

"I don't know. I guess it's possible."

"Mrs. McClain, do you own a small caliber handgun?"

"Yes."

"Do you know where it is now?"

"In my purse, where I always keep it."

"And where's your purse?"

"Up in room 313 on the nightstand by the bed."

"And you're sure, Mrs. McClain, that it couldn't be

anyplace else?"

"Yes, detective. I'm sure."

"Thing is that your purse was open and lying on the nightstand just as you say. We checked inside, and there was no gun. We did, however, find a small caliber 38-revolver lying next to the body in the bathroom."

"Detective, I don't like what you're insinuating about my wife," Booger said in an angry voice.

"I'm not accusing your wife of anything, Mr. McClain. Just asking questions."

"Mrs. McClain, did you throw anything away in the trash can next to the nightstand?"

"Maybe, I don't know. I don't remember."

"A note, maybe, something Mr. Williams may have given you?"

"No. I'm sure he didn't give me any sort of note or letter or anything of that nature."

"Detective, does my wife need a lawyer?"

"I don't see why she would, Mr. McClain. We're just having a conversation."

"Mrs. McClain, would you mind if I swabbed your hands? And your mouth?"

"Wait just a second, detective," Booger responded.

"Mr. McClain, I'm just trying to rule your wife out as a suspect. If she has nothing to hide, then she shouldn't object."

"It's fine, detective. Go ahead," Rose said.

"Mrs. McClain, would you have any reason to harm Mr. Williams?"

"My goodness, no. He was a sweet old man. We got along fine with him and certainly had no reason to harm him."

"What about your inheritance, Mrs. McClain? It's my

understanding that you inherited everything from Diane Landers' estate?"

"Yes, that's right."

"Odd, isn't it that she would leave everything to a friend that she had only known for a couple of months?"

"I guess. It certainly came as a surprise to me. I had no idea she had put me in her will, detective."

"Evidently, it was a surprise to her family, too."

"Wait, Jelks. I don't like what you're insinuating," Booger snapped.

"I'm not insinuating anything, McClain, just asking questions."

"Then are we free to go?"

"Yes, of course, just one more question, please. Are you aware, Mrs. McClain, that there are rumors of a second will, one that leaves the entirety of Diane Landers' estate to Cornilus, Brandon, and Ida Landers?"

"No, I'm not aware of that, detective."

"Are we free to go now?" Booger asked.

"Yes. But I'm afraid you're going to have to find another place to stay. The inn is a crime scene and will remain closed indefinitely. I'm also afraid that I can't let either of you back in your room. Your belongings will be taken to the police department, and I'll let you know when you can retrieve them."

"OK, detective."

"And Mr. and Mrs. McClain, leave me the address of where you'll be staying, and please don't leave town."

CHAPTER FOURTEEN
DEATH AT THE LANDERS THEATRE

For the first night in a while, Booger McClain slept like a baby. He was home and back in his own bed with no fear of ghosts or spirits or sounds in the night interrupting his sleep. He woke up refreshed, alert, and ready to take on the world that first morning back home. But for Rose, it was an entirely different story. She barely got any sleep. She tossed and turned and worried about the evidence that seemed to incriminate her in the murder of Bob Williams. Someone was setting her up. She was certain of it. But who? And why?

Those were questions that she had to find answers to.

Booger showered, dressed, and hurried to the kitchen. He could smell the aroma of fresh, strong Folgers coffee brewing.

He poured a cup of steaming hot, black coffee, took a sip, and walked over to the kitchen table to see his wife staring out the sliding glass door.

"What are you looking at?"

"Nothing really."

Booger had known his wife long enough to know when she was upset. Rose was the optimistic one. She always seemed to see the bright side of any situation. Her smile was contagious, and she was especially cheery in the morning. But not that day.

The detective looked at the empty bowl, jug of milk, and cereal box on the table in front of him and knew something was terribly wrong. His wife had always made him a hot meal or a fresh pastry in the morning. She had never forced him to eat a cold bowl of cereal.

"You're upset about last night and finding Bob Williams murdered in our bathroom?"

"Yes. And I'm worried that someone is trying to frame me for his murder."

"Yeah, I've thought about that, sweetie, and I think it has to be the Landers' siblings. Cornilus had a heated argument with Bob. He was upset over you inheriting everything in Diane's will, including Landers Theatre. Then add to that your announcement to Brandon and Ida that you were going to sell the theatre and not to them. I'd say you were pretty high on their shit list. Thing is, I just can't figure out why they would murder Bob."

"Whatever reason they had, I bet it has something to do with that basement," Rose said.

"And I intend to check it out. But first, I think we need to visit the Landers Theatre."

"Why?"

"Because whatever is going on has to involve both the Landers Theatre and the Walnut Street Inn. And you, sweetie, are the new owner of the theatre, so no one would be suspicious of you checking out your new property."

"OK."

Late that afternoon, the couple drove to Landers Theatre. The front door was locked, and a sign on the door read, *"All shows have been canceled, and the theatre will be closed until further notice."*

"Rose, did you have someone put that sign on the door?"

"No."

Rose unlocked the door and walked inside. The theatre was completely dark, with only the sunlight from outside shining through the front windows providing any light. The couple searched for a light switch and finally found one behind a wall curtain at the far end of the lobby. Rose flipped it on, but the lights did not come on.

"There's got to be an electrical box somewhere," Rose said.

"Down in the basement, most likely," Booger replied.

"Great, as if I'm not scared enough, you've got to take me down to a dark, frightening basement where God knows what could be lurking."

"You can stay here, Rose, if you want."

"No way. I'm coming with you, old man."

Booger pulled out his flashlight from his rear pocket, turned it on, and led his wife into the theatre to the door leading to the basement. With no windows to provide any sort of sunlight, the basement area was completely dark. He pointed his flashlight down the creaky old wooden stairs and started down with his wife following.

The basement was huge, several thousand square feet, containing dozens of shelves from floor to ceiling crowded with theater props, seasonal decorations, set backgrounds, and miscellaneous items. The floor contained large objects too big to fit on the shelves. There didn't appear to be much organization, as items were just left wherever there was room. In the corner of the basement on the right side was the office, spacious inside, containing one large oak desk and dozens of filing cabinets.

Ten feet to the left of the office was a small closet. Inside, it contained four electrical panels. Each one identified the area of the building that each fuse was for.

In three of the electrical boxes, the main power switch had been turned off. Booger turned them back on, and as he did, lights from upstairs began illuminating the area. When he flipped the master switch on the third box, the basement lights came on, and the detectives could see the enormity of the basement and the degree of clutter. Nearly every square inch of the basement was covered with items or shelves containing items.

When Booger opened the fourth electrical box, he saw something entirely different. The master switch in that box was still on.

"Well, there were lights on in part of the building," he commented to Rose.

The fuses in that box were titled "the fly tower" and "the upper circle."

"What does that mean, Booger?" Rose asked

"I have no idea, but if I were to guess, those areas are up high in the building."

"Do you think someone is up there? You know, because the switches in the electrical box haven't been turned off."

"I don't know, Rose, but I'm going to find out."

"I'll come with you."

"No. You stay here. Look through the desk and the filing cabinets. See if you can find any of the financial records or anything pertinent to the Landers family."

"How long are you going to be gone?"

"I don't know. I'll call you after I check everything out. Did you bring your spare gun?"

"Never leave home without one."

"OK, keep it handy. When I come back, I'll announce myself when I come down the stairs."

Before Booger left, he went to the closet with the electrical boxes, found the one for the Theatre and stage area, and flipped the main switch off. He hoped that with those lights off, it would make it easier for him to identify the "upper circle" and the "fly tower." That is, if someone didn't get wise to him coming and decide to turn those lights off.

With that, Booger gave his wife a kiss and headed up the stairs. There was an elevator just off the lobby that went up as far as the upper balcony. From there, he would have to take the stairs up as far as he could go, hoping that would take him to the "upper circle" or the "fly tower."

When the elevator door opened at the upper balcony, the entire theatre area was completely dark. In the distance, however, he could see some light. One area with light was just above and behind him, near the ceiling. The other light was coming from an area high above the stage. That light was some distance away from where he was standing.

Booger turned on his flashlight and pointed it around the sides and back of the balcony, looking for a stairway going up or a door that might lead to where he needed to go.

This was the first time that Booger had been inside Landers Theatre. It was huge, with three areas for seating: the orchestra and lower-level seating, the mezzanine, and the balcony. Booger was at the very top of the balcony, the nose-bleed seats, as he liked to call them. He was a long way from the stage.

The light above him appeared to be coming from a small room about twenty feet above the top of the upper balcony.

His flashlight spotted a door on the right-side wall about five rows down from the top row of seats. When he got to the door and tried to open it, he discovered it was locked. The detective used his best friend until the lock was released, and he was able to open the door.

Inside, old wooden stairs led up to another room. Again, it was locked, and again, he used his trusty metal tool to unlock it.

Booger lifted his gun, pointed it straight ahead, and

opened the door. Inside was a small room containing stage lighting equipment. No one was in the room, and there was no sign that anyone had been in the room recently.

There was one more area to check, the room above the stage. The stage area was a good distance from the back of the theatre, where Booger was, so he looked for any sort of hallway behind the walls of the theatre that would take him there faster.

On the opposite wall of the room from where Booger had entered was another door. It was unlocked, and when he opened it, there was a stairway leading down about twenty feet. This area appeared to be the guts of the building between the wall of the theatre and the brick siding of the facility. The wood stairs had aged with time and were cracked and loose and bent inward with every step. The outer wall was coated with spider webs, and rats scurried from one step to another.

At the bottom of the stairs was a dark walkway leading in the direction of the stage. The walkway was narrow, with loose floorboards.

Booger shined the light ahead and began walking slowly and carefully through the narrow, dark walkway. In places, the floorboards were missing and gave way to a large opening that appeared to go all the way down to the basement. The detective shined his light down one opening in the floor and couldn't see how far down it went. One thing he was certain of, though, was that one misstep could cost him his life.

At the end of the walkway to the left was a door opening to the back of the stage, dressing rooms, and a staging area. Straight ahead, about ten feet past that door, were stairs leading up and a sign marked "fly tower" with an arrow pointing up the stairs. Unlike the wooden stairs in other parts of the theater, these steps were made of concrete and much steeper, going up at least thirty feet to the top of the stage area. A door at the top of the stairs opened to a large area that contained scenery and backgrounds, and numerous pulleys and ropes to lower scenery to the stage during set changes. The lights were on in the fly tower, but no one was there.

At the rear of the fly tower area was another door with a "do not enter" sign on it. That door was locked. Booger used his tool friend to unlock it. He raised his gun straight ahead and opened the door.

Inside was what appeared to be a small apartment. It had a living room with furniture and a television. The television was on, but the volume was turned off. On a coffee table in front of an old brown sofa was an ashtray with a half-smoked cigarette, and next to that was a coffee mug containing about half a cup of coffee still warm.

In the kitchen area, dirty dishes were in the sink, and freshly made coffee was in the pot of a coffeemaker. An open newspaper was spread over the breakfast table. Food was in the refrigerator, and the cabinets were stocked with food and dishes.

Lights were on throughout the apartment.

Booger walked past the kitchen into a hallway. On the left was a bathroom. Inside, the curtain hanging over the bathtub was closed. The detective raised his gun again as he pulled the curtain back. No one was there, but the tub was wet. Someone had been there and not very long ago.

Booger checked the bedroom closet. Men's clothes were hanging inside. He checked the dresser drawers. Men's socks, underwear, pajamas, and shirts were there. Since Ida and Brandon had been staying at the Bed and Breakfast the past several nights, Booger speculated that Cornilus Landers may have occupied that apartment. But where was he now?

Rose looked through every filing cabinet in the office. Most of the files contained employee information and records. There were files for vendors and for past and upcoming shows. And there were no financial records.

A locked drawer on the desk got Rose's attention. With the help of a straightened paper clip, Rose was able to release the lock. Inside it, she found a black leather-bound notebook that contained dates, dollar amounts, numbers, and initials. They appeared to be transactions of some sort, one every week, based on the dates listed. Each occurring on a Sunday, it appeared. Rose grabbed the notebook and put it in her purse.

Also, in the drawer was a one-page legal document, a will. It had today's date on it and was signed by Cornilus Landers. The other signature on it was that of Rose. Faked signature, obviously, but not a bad forgery. The document had not been notarized yet. The Will stated that in the event of Rose's death, the Landers Theatre and all of Diane Landers' inherited wealth would pass on to Cornilus Landers.

Rose picked up her cell phone and called her husband. "Booger, you need to get down here as soon as possible. I found something that you need to see."

But Booger couldn't hear everything his wife had said. "Rose, you're breaking up. What do you want?"

Rose shouted into the phone. "Get down here right away, old man. I need you."

This time, she came through loud and clear. Booger moved his cell phone away from his ear. "Geez, Rose, you didn't have to shout. I'll be there right away."

Rose took pictures of the will with her cell phone when she heard the basement door open, followed by footsteps coming down the old, wooden steps.

"That's too quick for it to be Booger," she thought.

As the steps got closer to the office, Rose couldn't help herself and yelled out, "Is that you, Booger?"

There was no answer.

She pulled the small handgun from her purse and raised it toward the door.

Rose listened intently as the footsteps got closer, then stopped. She sensed that someone was just outside the office door.

Then, the footsteps started up again, going past the office and farther into the basement.

Rose heard another door open, and then all the lights went dark. Rose could barely hear the footsteps moving again over her beating heart.

She steadied her gun as she heard the footsteps stop directly in front of her office door.

Blinded by the dark, she listened intently for any sound of the office door opening. She heard what sounded like the turning of the knob. "Booger, is that you?" she shouted one more time. There was no response.

Then she heard the soft squeaking of the door hinges as the door began to open. "I've got a gun," she warned.

After silently counting to three and consumed by fear in the pitch-black office, she fired the gun, one, two, three times.

She heard the sound of a body falling to the floor.

Rose, body shaking and heart racing, fell into the chair.

Still in shock, Rose didn't hear her husband running down the basement stairs and calling out to her.

Her eyes needed a few seconds to adjust to the light once Booger had turned the lights back on at the fuse box. She closed her eyes, rubbed them, and then reopened them to see her husband hurrying into the office, kneeling down to check the pulse of the body on the floor.

"He's dead," he announced to his wife.

"Who is it?" Rose said to Booger as she tried to adjust to the light.

"It's Cornilus Landers."

CHAPTER FIFTEEN
CONSEQUENCES

"Before the police arrive, sweetie, did you find anything in the office?"

"Yes, in my purse, a notebook," Rose answered with her voice cracking.

Booger opened Rose's purse and pulled out a small, black notebook. Inside were dates, all Sundays, nearly one every week. Also, there were dollar amounts, hundreds of thousands of dollars each week. Next to that was an abbreviation. Booger scrolled down to see K.C., STL, and DEN. They appeared to be abbreviations of cities. Next to that were the names, Sam, Lou, Tommy.

The detective had no idea what the book was for, but he was certain it was important, so he put the small leather book in his pocket.

"Was there anything else you found?" he asked.

His wife lifted her cell phone and showed her husband the pictures of the forged will.

"Damn, Rose. This doesn't look good. It's forged, obviously. But whoever did this certainly has a reason to do away with you, and it appears that person is Cornilus Landers, which doesn't make any sense because he's dead. Unless that's what someone planned. With your signature on it, someone could make an argument that you were coerced into signing it, and that would give you motive for killing Cornilus."

"Shit," Rose replied.

"Where is the actual document, Rose?"

"It's in the drawer of the desk."

That's when Booger heard the sirens of police cars outside.

He tried desperately to open the drawer, but it was jammed. He used his hands, then his trusty metal friend, to try to pry the door open, but it wouldn't budge.

Within minutes, it seemed a half dozen squad cars, an ambulance, the coroner, and a CSI unit, followed closely behind by three television trucks, converged on the Landers Theatre. Murders were rare occurrences in Springfield, particularly ones as high-profile as Cornilus Landers.

When Booger heard footsteps coming down the stairs, he stopped trying to pry open the drawer. Detective Walter Jelks was the first officer on the scene. After doing a cursory examination of the body, he turned the scene over to his CSI team. Then, he ordered his officers to separate Booger and Rose before his interrogation of both.

After hearing Rose's story, he went to Booger. "I'm sorry, McClain, but this doesn't look good for your wife."

"Just a minute, detective, you can't be suggesting that Rose did anything other than defend herself."

"Defend herself? McClain, Cornilus Landers didn't even have a weapon on him. Your wife shot an unarmed man, a man who had every right to be in the theater."

"Detective, Rose fired the Landers siblings. She had no idea Cornilus Landers was here. Rose was in fear for her life. The lights were turned off in the basement. She heard footsteps. Rose asked who was there. He didn't respond. When he opened the office door, and with the lights out, she had no idea if the intruder was armed or not."

"So, she took it upon herself to shoot whoever came through that door?"

"Yes, and I would have done the same under similar circumstances."

"Let me ask you, McClain, how do I know the basement lights were off when Landers came through that door?"

"Because I told you, detective. When I came downstairs, it was completely dark in the basement. I went to the fuse box to turn on the lights."

"So, you say. I do find it curious that you would go to the fuse box before checking on your wife."

"Because she said that she was alright. I wanted the lights on so I could see what happened and so I could see who broke into the office."

"So, you say. McClain, did you know there was a second will in that desk drawer?"

"No."

"It was signed by your wife giving Landers Theatre over to Cornilus Landers in the event of her death. You know what I think, McClain?"

"I have no idea."

"I think your wife and Cornilus Landers were in this office together, and I think Mr. Landers coerced your wife to sign that will. That would certainly give her a motive for killing him."

"Detective, I don't like your attitude."

"Well then, you certainly aren't going to like what I'm going to say next."

"What?"

"Your wife is under arrest."

Detective Walker Jelks walked over to Rose, read her

rights, put handcuffs on her, and began to walk her out.

Booger yelled to his wife, "Don't say anything, Rose. I'll get you an attorney."

Rose, a person who had never been arrested and never even gotten a speeding ticket before, was led out of the theater and put in the back of a police car as dozens of onlookers and two camera crews watched closely.

That night, she would be booked and put in a cell at the Greene County jail.

As promised, Booger got Rose a lawyer – the best criminal defense attorney in Springfield, in fact, Nancy Price-Young. The next morning, in front of Judge William Caldwell, the bright, attractive middle-aged attorney argued for reasonable bail for her client. Booger was in the courtroom, prepared to pay whatever it took to bring his wife home.

But murders were rare in Springfield, and Corneilus Landers was about as high-profile a murder victim as the conservative judge had ever had. To make matters worse, it was an election year. The judge refused bail.

Booger smiled at his wife and told her everything would be alright as she was led away from the courtroom.

Her husband had never seen that look on Rose's face before. Hurt, dispirited, and embarrassed. Rose was not one to ever seek attention, and now it seemed the entire city was focused on her. She knew that she was innocent, but there wasn't a damn thing she could do about it. If there was a glimmer of hope, it was that Booger knew she was innocent, too, and was determined to uncover the truth.

It just didn't make sense to Booger that Corneilus would come down to the basement unarmed, turn out the lights, and open the door to the office with Rose inside, warning him to announce himself. It was similar to suicide-by-cop, with Rose being the cop. He had to know she was armed. Rose announced it. It was as if he wanted to be shot.

That brown leather notebook with dates, amounts, city abbreviations, and names had to be the key to what the Landers' siblings were up to. There had to be plenty of secrets in that theater, and Booger was determined to find them.

That night, the detective went back to the scene, knowing in his heart the answers to unlocking the oddities surrounding Cornelius' death had to be there.

It was a cloudy, rainy night, a good night not to be seen. If anyone was inside, the sound of heavy rain and thunder would numb any noise Booger made breaking into the theater.

Yellow police tape surrounded much of the building. Doors were locked, chained, and had signs warning people that it was a crime scene and no one was permitted inside.

The detective looked for a window on the side and back of the building. Most were too high for him to climb into. The ones on the ground giving light to the basement had bars on them to prevent people from gaining entrance. However, at the rear of the theater, covered mainly by bushes and overgrown weeds, was a hinged metal door with a simple lock. Booger broke the lock and opened the door.

The door opened to an angled tunnel. Booger shined his flashlight inside. He could not see the end of the tunnel, which was about two feet wide by two feet high. The tunnel appeared to be an old coal chute, probably used many years ago when the theater used coal to feed the furnace.

The detective was borderline claustrophobic, many times opting to take the stairs rather than an elevator. The thought of pushing his large, framed body down a narrow, dark chute that he couldn't even see the end of sent chills down his spine.

It was true love for his wife and the fact that the chute appeared to be his only option to enter the building that motivated him to say the Lord's Prayer and climb in. He closed his eyes and let go of the top edge of the tunnel sending him careening down the twisting chute twenty feet to the basement floor, landing hard on the most cushioned part of his body, his butt.

Once inside, he got to his feet, turned his flashlight back on, and began a search of the basement. That would not be an easy endeavor in the dark, with only the aid of a narrow beam of light from his flashlight, given the enormity of that basement, densely populated with seasonal decorations, set props, and miscellaneous items.

In talking to his wife after the shooting, Rose said she heard one set of footsteps coming down the stairs and walking past her office just before the lights went out. If the person walking down the stairs was Corneilus Landers, then why did he go directly to the closet to turn off the breaker, causing the basement to go dark? He didn't have a gun. At least the police didn't find a gun, so was his intention only to frighten Rose? If so, when his wife announced she was armed, why didn't he back off? He had to know that it was likely she would fire that gun in self-defense when he opened the door.

Booger couldn't make sense of what happened. But he hoped that he could find some clues in that basement.

It was completely dark and eerily quiet in the basement. The lights were off, and the rain and thunder from outside had slowed and were silenced by the depth underground and the enormity of the basement.

With his flashlight guiding the way, the detective moved past the office to the closet with the electrical panels. He turned on the breaker in the fourth box, and the large fluorescent lights in the ceiling began to slowly turn on.

With the lights on, he could clearly see the rows and rows of metal shelving. All appeared to be nearly full of random items with no rational organization to them. Christmas decorations, painted backdrops, and set décor all mixed together. *"How did anyone find what they were looking for?"* Booger wondered.

Suddenly, a large rat the size of a small cat scurried past him on the floor. The basement was a maze of shelving so full that some decorations sat on the floor with no space to put them on the shelves. The whole area reminded Booger of a murder case he investigated years earlier in the house of a hoarder. Nearly every square inch of the small ranch home was covered with trash and remnants of the past that most people would have gotten rid of long ago.

This basement was like that, cluttered, unorganized, and smelling of mold, staleness, and age. Everything he saw appeared to be remnants of the past whose life was no longer useful.

Coming out of another row of shelving, he caught something moving quickly ahead, staying in his eyesight for only a split second, too little time to determine what it was. But it was large. He could tell it was large.

Booger hated that he couldn't tell what had flashed so quickly before his eyes. Whatever it was had unnerved him. His right hand trembled slightly as he moved forward through the rows of shelving.

His nerves would relax when he came out of one row and spotted a walkway. *"Perhaps it went down here,"* he thought.

With no idea what he was looking for, Booger continued on the walkway toward the rear of the basement.

Suddenly, the lights in the basement went dark, and

Booger knew for sure he was not alone. He turned his flashlight back on and used the narrow beam of light to guide him farther into the basement.

His hair began to stand up on the back of his neck when he heard weird sounds straight ahead. The sounds were like something was moving about, not walking, more like shuffling or dragging its feet twenty, maybe thirty feet ahead, but coming closer.

Suddenly, at the edge of the beam of light, something appeared. It was large, maybe eight feet tall, but just far enough away that he couldn't make out what it was.

His hand shook as he turned off the flashlight. Whoever or whatever was there, he didn't want to see him. Then Booger moved quickly to his left and behind some metal shelving in an attempt to hide from whatever or whoever was sharing that basement with him.

Booger's heart raced as he bent down behind a cold metal shelf and listened intently for the sound of something moving closer. The dragging noise continued, with the sound getting louder with every movement closer to the detective. Ten feet away, he guessed.

Suddenly, the sound stopped. The detective waited and listened for several moments. The dragging sound was gone.

Finally, the detective, convinced that whatever it was had gone, stood up, lifted his flashlight, and turned it back on.

That's when he dropped the flashlight and nearly fell to the ground. Very seldom in his life had Booger been truly frightened. This was one of those times when his heart nearly beat out of his chest, and cold chills ran through his body.

In front of him, not a foot away and staring directly into his eyes, was the Kangaroo man, a sort of half man, half kangaroo with the face of a man and the tail of a kangaroo with long furry feet that shuffled as it walked.

Booger was frozen in fear. The kangaroo man began to smile, teeth long, big, and sharp. Suddenly, Booger felt a warmth come over him, a familiar, comfortable feeling that told the old man that he had nothing to fear.

That's when he recognized the oddity. The kangaroo man was Samuel, the man from heaven who had sent him back to Rose, the mercurial man kicked out of the City of Gold, whom Booger met when he almost died investigating an abandoned mental hospital. In that instant, Booger realized that Samuel was either there to end his life and take him back to the other side, or he was there to help.

Samuel didn't say a word. He simply pointed in the northeast direction of the basement. Then he disappeared.

"Well, that was helpful," Booger said out loud. The basement of that theater was enormous, large enough to fit two football fields inside.

It was obvious to the detective that Samuel wanted him to find something or someone. *"But why?"* Booger thought.

He turned the flashlight in the direction that Samuel had pointed and began walking. That basement was dark, cold, and eerie. The only sounds heard were his own footsteps and an occasional growl from an old furnace. Every so often, he could hear the squeal of a rat scurrying past him or the crunch of a roach as he stepped on it. Spiders clung to their low-hanging webs as Booger's head collided with them. Then, just thirty feet from where he encountered the kangaroo man, the detective heard the squealing sound of rats, lots of rats. The sound intensified as Booger moved closer.

Then, the beam of his flashlight caught dozens of rats

feasting on something on the floor near a wall. As he came close, the rats scurried away, and he could see something on the floor. He shined his flashlight down to his feet. It was a large puddle of liquid. *"It wasn't water,"* he thought. *"Too thick, too dark."*

He bent down and dipped his finger in it. Then, he took a taste with his tongue and spit it out. It was blood. He was certain. It was pooled on the floor.

Booger took three steps beyond the pool of blood, and suddenly, the kangaroo man appeared again. This time, there was no smile. He simply pointed north and then disappeared. The detective continued walking in that direction. The unorganized clutter soon gave way to a clear walkway, rows of shelving to his left, and a wall to his right. There was a three-foot-wide path of open space straight ahead heading north.

Without any obstacles, other than an occasional rat, roach, or spider web, to impede his journey, Booger moved at a quicker pace while still being cognizant of his surroundings.

He thought it was odd that Samuel would turn the lights out in the basement if he wanted to help. *"None of this makes sense. Am I losing my mind? Have I had a stroke?"*

Soon, he would reach the northern wall of the basement. There, the walkway made a sharp left toward the east. He followed the path another thirty yards or so before he encountered the east wall. There, he shined his light forward and discovered an opening in the wall, a tunnel.

"This must be what Samuel wanted me to find," he thought.

That's when he heard footsteps behind him. Booger crouched down behind a shelf, hoping that whoever was coming wouldn't discover him. A minute later, Booger watched as four feet went past him down the walkway. They didn't spot him.

The two men went into the hole in the wall, and soon, their

footsteps couldn't be heard. Booger decided to follow them.

The tunnel was almost tall and wide enough for him to stand, maybe six feet tall by three feet wide, dug out of the earth. It was a dirt tunnel with reinforced wood beams to strengthen its walls and ceiling. It was completely dark inside, with the detective's only visibility coming from the flashlight's narrow beam of light.

Booger pointed the flashlight straight ahead, lowered his head so as not to hit the wood beams bracing the ceiling, and then moved ahead into the tunnel.

The tunnel moved downward from the basement, maybe ten feet or so, then leveled off. About thirty feet past the entrance, Booger could smell fresh air, clean, almost like pure oxygen, blowing into the tunnel from up above. He shined the flashlight above and saw an air vent.

Another thirty yards into the tunnel, there was another air vent, and 30 yards past that, another.

It was a sophisticated tunnel built underneath a busy section of the city. Booger had been in the cave system that runs beneath Springfield before, but this wasn't that. This was all human-built. It had a purpose, but Booger had no idea what that purpose was, but he had a feeling that if he kept following those two men at a distance, he would soon find out.

CHAPTER SIXTEEN
THE TUNNEL

The only tunnels in Springfield that Booger was aware of were in the northwest section of the city near downtown. But those manmade tunnels spanned from natural caverns deep underneath the city. Those caverns were used to store and cool beer in the period before refrigeration. Tunnels were built to house and deliver the beer from two breweries in the city. Those tunnels had a purpose, but it was a legal purpose.

Booger suspected this tunnel had a nefarious purpose.

As he ventured deeper in, the tunnel just kept going. It went on for at least a mile, he figured, going down into the earth in some spots and rising closer to the surface in others, all the time maintaining the same height and width and including air vents every thirty yards or so.

"Someone, some people, must have spent years building it at a great cost," Booger thought.

Up ahead, Booger heard a sound. He turned off his flashlight and stood still. The sound was in the distance and muffled. *"People,"* he thought, *"But too far away to make out any words."*

He speculated that they were the two men from the basement and hoped they didn't spot the beam of his flashlight.

With the flashlight off, Booger was completely blind in that tunnel. He moved to his left and reached his hand out to touch the side of the tunnel. He would use that wall to guide him ahead.

Slowly and quietly, he moved on. A few yards ahead, the wall began to dip. But this dip was different. It was at a much steeper angle than other times. The tunnel was going much deeper into the earth. The decline was steep and long. When it leveled off, Booger had no idea how far underground he was. Then he heard the sound of air blowing from above. It was a constant flow of oxygen blowing down on him.

The sound of people talking was louder now, just above a whisper and less muffled. He could make out a few words, but not many. The more he moved forward, the louder and more distinct the voices became. That's when he heard the two men talking about the lights being on in the basement and that they suspected a stranger had been down there, but they hadn't seen anyone. "Maybe he is gone," one of the men speculated.

Suddenly, the conversation stopped, and Booger heard a door open and close.

Another ten yards and the voices came back, but somewhat muffled. He moved to his right, touching the other wall and feeling around with his right hand. Suddenly, he felt the dirt wall change to metal. The voices were coming from behind that metal. He felt around the metal, locating a small opening that went vertically from the floor nearly up to the ceiling, then moving horizontally three feet or so, then moving downward vertically. It was a door. Damn, he hated being blinded by the dark.

To the left of the door was what felt like a keypad. Booger put his ear next to the door, hoping to make out whatever conversation was going on inside. He heard several voices, men and women. But he couldn't hear enough to understand what they were talking about.

Suddenly, light illuminated the tunnel, piercing his eyes that had endured darkness for the last hour. The light blinded him. He rubbed his eyes and tried desperately to get them to focus. For several seconds, he couldn't see and had to remain still.

When his sight began to come back, he could see a long tunnel ahead and then angling to the left. Footsteps were coming, and three large shadows appeared on the tunnel wall about fifty feet ahead in the area where it veered to the left.

Whoever was coming would certainly see him anytime now. Booger turned and ran. There was a place ahead where the tunnel veered to the right. With luck, he could make it to that area before they saw him.

Ten feet, five feet away, and then he would turn to the right and be out of sight. Finally, he was there, panting, and with his heart racing, he prayed the people coming did not see him.

The detective waited for a minute or so, and not hearing footsteps, he peeped around the corner just to see three figures going into the room behind the metal door. Their backs were turned, and they were too far away to see clearly, but based on the long brown hair of one of the people, he assumed at least one of them was a woman.

When the metal door closed, Booger began his journey to the other side of the tunnel again. Past the door and down the corridor until it veered to the left. With the lights on, he could see the sophistication of the tunnel clearly. Vents from above blew fresh air down every ten feet or so now. The dirt floor and walls were replaced with concrete, and bright fluorescent lights shone from above. The walls widened, and the ceiling was higher, so much so that Booger could stand fully and still have plenty of room above his head. The area had changed from a primitive walkway to a comfortable hallway wide enough for two to three people to walk side by side.

Thirty feet past the turn in the tunnel was a steel door on the right wall. Booger stopped and listened to hear if anyone was inside. There were no sounds. It, too, had a keypad, and the door was locked. He tried in vain to force through his best friend, but it was clear quickly that the only way to open the door was by using the right combination of numbers on the keypad.

Booger then reached into his pocket and pulled out his Swiss Army multi-tool pocketknife. He used a thin screwdriver to wedge inside the small opening behind the keypad and against the wall. *"If he could remove the keypad, maybe he could cut the wires and short-circuit the keypad so he could open the door,"* he thought.

He worked to drive the metal head of the screwdriver into the opening. When it was far enough in, he leveraged it against the wall to pry the face of the keypad loose. With the face of the keypad dangling from the wall, he noticed three wires leading from the keypad into the wall.

One by one, he cut the wires. After the third one was cut, Booger heard a clicking sound. He put the face of the keypad back on the wall, giving the appearance that it was still operational. Then he tried the door handle. It turned, and the door opened.

Inside, the room was dark. He used his flashlight to check the inside walls for a light switch. When he found one just to the left of the door, he flipped it on. Fluorescent lights above flickered and then began to come on. In a few seconds, the room was bright.

The room smelled of bleach. The walls and floor were white. It was clean, almost sterile, and reminded Booger of a hospital operating room. There was a large table to the right, which had dozens of surgical tools on it.

That was when he noticed the beds. Ten of them lined against the far wall, simple steel beds with a thin mattress. Attached to the wall on each side of every bed were what looked like shackles, metal chains with handcuffs on the end, and embedded in the wall. There was another shackle attached to the bottom of every bed.

On another wall was a simple toilet, out in the open and not hidden by any walls. A sink was next to it. A cabinet next to it was locked. It was a simple lock that took Booger less than fifteen seconds to pry open. Inside the cabinet were a variety of needles and syringes. Next to it was a small refrigerator containing dozens of vials of liquid, medication, Booger assumed.

"People who were brought into this room did not come voluntarily. It was not a room anyone wanted to be in." Booger thought.

He knew the room that he had encountered earlier also had a purpose, but Booger did not go in there because it had people in it. He would need to go back when it was empty. Perhaps seeing what was in that room might help him understand what dark purpose this room had. At this point, he was only getting a few pieces of the puzzle.

In the far-left corner of the room was another door. It, too, was locked, but he was able to pry it open. The room was the size of a closet, with no windows. It was cold, freezing cold inside, and then he got a whiff of a terrible odor. He had smelled that odor before. It was the smell of death, rotting flesh. He took a picture of both rooms on his cell phone. Then it was time to leave.

Booger McClain turned out the lights, opened the door, and began walking down the tunnel to the other side, anxious to find out where the tunnel went to.

It wasn't far, thirty to forty feet away. Booger reached the end of the tunnel, and in front of him was a large door, about five feet wide and seven feet tall, with a handle. Like the other doors, a keypad was on the wall just to the left of it. The detective pulled out his multi-tool pocket knife again and removed the face of the keypad, then cut the wires. He heard a clicking noise coming from the door and turned the doorknob. He opened it slowly.

On the other side was a basement – a cellar that was completely dark inside. The detective took two steps in, lifted his flashlight, and turned it on. That's when he saw her.

And she saw him. Standing ten feet away with a 30-caliber revolver pointing directly at him was Sue Williams.

"I see you're feeling better now, Sue," Booger said with a nervous smile on his face.

"With your left hand, reach into your holster and take out the gun," Sue said calmly. "Then roll it to me."

He did exactly as she asked.

"Now, lay down on the ground, McClain," she ordered. "Cup your hands above your head."

"Well, Mrs. Williams, I didn't expect to see you here. Can I assume your husband is somewhere close by?"

She didn't say anything, just walked a few feet to one of the walls and flipped a light switch on. Then she pulled a cell phone from her pocket, dialed a number, and when someone answered, she said, "I've got Booger McClain in the basement. Please come and get him."

Booger lifted his head to get a look at the cellar and realized he was underneath the Walnut Street Inn. With the lights on, it was the first time he was able to see the entirety of the basement. It was a relatively small area, maybe forty feet long by thirty feet wide, with walls of cinder blocks and a dirt and gravel floor. On one side was a freight elevator. Near it were stairs leading up. In one corner was a large furnace. Next to it were two large water heaters. Then he saw it. Only about ten feet away was an area of the floor, completely free of gravel, with only fresh dirt and what looked like an area that had been dug up recently. From the size of the dirt piles, it looked like several graves.

"Can I ask you a question, Mrs. Williams?"

"Please call me Sue."

"Okay, Sue. What brings you back to the inn? I mean, you were in the hospital the last I knew."

"Yeah, food poisoning. Imagine your brother-in-law trying to kill you. Bob was never too bright. He certainly didn't know how much poison to use. It just made me a little sick. As you can see, I'm as good as new now."

"Did you murder Bob?"

"No, are you crazy? I couldn't harm a fly," he said with a smile.

"That revolver in your hand says differently."

"Maybe you're right."

"So why come back here after the murder with police tape outside? Don't you fear the cops will come back and find you here?"

"No, I believe Brandon has taken care of that."

"You haven't answered my question. Why come back here?"

"Oh, don't you know Mr. McClain? My husband and I are the new owners of the Walnut Street Inn, and we plan on re-opening it very soon."

"Aren't you rushing it a bit? Doesn't the business pass on to your sister-in-law? After all, she was married to the deceased."

"You're quite right, Mr. McClain. The ownership would have passed on to Cindy. However, just yesterday, she signed over the inn to my husband and me."

"Well, that must have cost you a pretty penny."

"Actually, 100 pretty pennies. We paid her one dollar for the business."

"And what would motivate her to give up a nice bed and breakfast for a dollar?"

"Grief over the loss of her husband, I suppose, and possibly not wanting to join poor Bob in the afterlife, at least not right away."

"Yes, fear is a good motivator," he said, wondering as he spoke how he might keep the conversation going so she wasn't using her pistol. "I don't suppose you could tell me the purpose of that tunnel and the two rooms inside it?"

"Well, I'd like to, but, unfortunately, I stay out of my husband's business. And what happens in that tunnel is certainly my husband's business. However, I'm sure he won't have any problem enlightening you the next time you see him, considering you won't be living much longer."

The door of the tunnel began to open, and that distracted Sue for a brief second, just enough time for Booger to lunge toward her, knocking her gun out of her hand. The detective grabbed the revolver and ran up the stairs toward the first floor of the inn. As he did, Booger heard the woman scream out, "He's heading upstairs."

As he opened the door to the first floor of the bed and breakfast, Booger stopped dead in his tracks. Standing in front of him, less than five feet away, was Brandon Landers, pointing a 22-caliber revolver directly at him.

"Nice try, Mr. McClain. Now let's go back down."

Booger, defeated, turned around and walked slowly back down the stairs where Pat Williams was waiting for him.

The two men walked the detective back to the tunnel and

down to the room with the beds and chains. There, he was taken to a separate room about the size of a closet. Inside was a wooden plank about two feet wide and six feet long, welded upright to the wall with three thick leather straps attached to each side. There, he was handcuffed and his legs were tied together. Then he was strapped upright to the wooden bed with all three leather straps, one at his chest, another at his waist, and the third just below his knees. The straps were tightened so tightly that he couldn't move.

After securing Booger, Pat left the room, leaving only Brandon Landers inside the small room with the detective.

"Smells like death in here," Booger said. "You should really open up some windows."

"Mr. McClain, you and your wife have caused quite a bit of trouble. What do you think we should do with you?"

"I'd call the police and have them pick me up."

"No, I don't think so. I've got another plan for you. But first, tell me, does anyone else know you're here?"

"Yes, several people. Do you think I'd be crazy enough to come here alone and not tell others where I'd be?"

"Yes, I do."

"Can I ask you a question, Landers?"

"Sure."

"Was it you who killed your brother?"

"Yes. Didn't want to, but I figured it was better to kill him before he killed me. I loved my brother, but the man was a greedy asshole. He wasn't satisfied splitting the profits in thirds, so I figured sooner or later, he was going to get rid of me and my sister. Besides, I needed to frame your wife."

"What about Bob Williams. Who killed him?"

"Cornilus. Bob was a softy. He didn't see a great

opportunity ahead of him. So, Cornilus thought there was a need for new management at the inn, more cooperative management. We can't have all our little secrets coming to the surface, can we? And, well, if you could kill Bob and frame your wife for his death, that was even better. But when the police refused to arrest your wife for Bob's murder, we just had to look for another option. Cornilus made the most sense. He was a greedy bastard, and Ida and I were convinced he would kill us as soon as he had an opportunity."

"So how did you pull it off, I mean, getting my wife to shoot Cornilus?"

"It was pretty ingenious if I say so myself. I had help from Ida. She cooked him a wonderful last meal and laced a glass of wine with arsenic. I've got to say poisoning isn't the most pleasant way to die, but it seemed to do the trick. Ten minutes after drinking it, the old man was gone. Then, it was a matter of getting him downstairs. For that, I had the help of Pat and Randolph. Remember Randolph, the kid who ran the front desk. It seems young Randolph has a bit of a drug problem. He'll do almost anything to keep his habit going. The two of them carried my brother from the apartment above the stage all the way down to the basement. That was when he started to wake up. Damn brother turned out to be harder to kill than we thought, or perhaps my sister didn't put enough arsenic in his wine. Regardless, Pat finished him off by smashing the back of his skull with a hammer. They propped him up against one of the walls in the basement. We didn't really know what to do with him until you and your wife broke into the theater. When your wife came down to the basement, we put a plan in place to frame her for the murder. When that office door began to open, your wife had no idea that she was shooting a man who was already dead."

"Why frame her?"

"Because she took what was rightfully ours. Our niece's fortune was supposed to go to her only living family, not to some stranger who happened to befriend her shortly before she died. She really ruined our plans."

"You killed Diane Landers, too, didn't you?"

"No, Mr. McClain. That was my dear departed older brother. We were afraid she was going to uncover our lucrative business, and we couldn't have that. Even knowing that, we gave her an opportunity to join us in the business as a full partner with 25 percent ownership. It was worth tens of millions of dollars every year. But, as you might've guessed, she turned us down and threatened to go to the police and expose our operation. Well, that sealed her fate. Cornilus, being the psychopath he was, took on the task of getting rid of dear Diane. She was dead long before that tumble down the stairs.

"So, Cornilus killed her just before she brought someone in to examine the books."

"Brandon laughed. "Come on, Mr. McClain, I would have expected a detective with your reputation to be smarter than that. The books had nothing to do with it. Sure, a good CPA would have found discrepancies, but not on a large scale. The Landers Theater was profitable, but it was mostly a cover for other businesses. The theatre was a means to an end, just like the bed and breakfast. We need to control both so that our underground business stays secret. My brother was afraid Diane would follow through with her threat and go to the police, exposing our operation. We pay a good penny for police protection, but she might talk to the wrong person. The majority of the Springfield police are honest cops. We couldn't take that chance."

"So, how do these tunnels and tables and shackles make

you money?"

"Take a guess, Mr. McClain."

"Well, from the looks of this room, I would say prostitution."

"Close, but no cigar. I guess you could say we're into providing cheap labor. You ever seen a South American Gold Mine, Mr. McClain?"

"No."

"Well, it's a very lucrative business. The thing is, it is very labor-intensive. And labor doesn't come cheap unless, of course, you can find a way to cut those costs. That's where we come in. Oh, and it's not just Gold Mines. We provide cheap labor for other businesses, too, businesses that tend to need disposable labor, so to speak. Our clients pay us a flat cost, and we provide them as many workers as they need."

"Slaves, you mean?"

"Now, Mr. McClain, 'slaves' has such a negative connotation. We prefer to refer to the workers as disposable labor."

"Whatever you call them, people just don't disappear without someone asking questions."

"You'd be surprised, McClain. There are a lot of lost souls out there – people that no one cares about. People estranged from their families or without families altogether. You know, drug addicts, prostitutes, the homeless. People that no one will miss."

"But how do you lure them to you?"

"Not to me, McClain. To the theater and to the inn. It's amazing what desperate people will do for a free meal, a bath, some new clothes, and a safe place to spend the night. We even throw in some entertainment once in a while. Did you know the Landers Theatre has a special section of free seats for the needy?

We give those poor souls a wonderful last night before they are sent off to one of our clients. It's a good front because even if they escape somehow, they're never going to assume that it was us, the people who helped them, that carried them off into the night under ski masks. Yes, human trafficking is quite profitable, and The Order has all the connections."

"The Order?! Of course."

"That's right. Yes, you're a detective who's been around long enough to know that The Order always has its hands in such matters. And guess what? They have an open bounty on you, McClain. I'll get paid handsomely for your head on a platter."

Booger had been chasing The Order his whole career. It was an elusive crime boss syndicate that seemed to be behind every unsolved case the detective investigated. It was like a dark cloud that hung over his life, and like a cloud, he could never quite touch it.

"So that accounts for this room. What is the other larger room down the tunnel used for?"

"Heroin, Mr. McClain. Did you know that there are a tremendous number of poppy fields in South America and that many of the owners of gold mines also own poppy fields? Many of our clients for whom we provide labor find it more advantageous to pay us in heroin instead of cash. And, sometimes, we're happy to take poppy seeds themselves – depending on the arrangement. In that room, we take the poppy seeds and make opium, morphine, and heroin. That business has been very good to us."

"I get that the tunnel system connects the bed and breakfast to the theater, but both of those are legitimate businesses. Regular people go to the theater and the inn. Isn't it dangerous to have an illegal operation right under their noses?"

"The fact that the inn and the theater are real businesses is why this works. Our operation is hidden in plain sight, so to speak. Plus, those businesses make money too. We want the theater and the inn to be profitable. Money is money. We don't want to interfere with that. It's just that we make more money selling drugs and moving people through The Order. Plus, it's easy to say we're renovating a room here or there or that the inn is full, and there is a lot of downtime at the theater, too. We've got the perfect setup, and that's why we couldn't have Diane or your wife involved – neither could be trusted."

Suddenly, the door to the room opened, and Pat walked in. "It's ready," he said to Brandon.

"Well, I'm afraid that is all the time we have, McClain," Brandon said.

"One last question for Mr. Williams, please. How long have you and your wife been involved in the business?"

"Ever since the beginning, we've handled the travel arrangements for the labor and the poppy. You see, living in St. Louis gives us certain advantages in moving people and products in and out. When you're doing work for The Order, you have to be able to move product and people quickly, and big cities are helpful for that. Springfield is just one tiny cog in a much bigger wheel."

"Yeah, I'm well aware."

"Now that you have all your answers, McClain, you can go to your afterlife satisfied," Brandon said with an evil laugh as both men left the room and locked the door behind them.

A minute later, Booger heard a hissing sound and saw smoke coming out of a vent in the ceiling. The smell made him cough. Soon, he began to choke. Soon, his throat tightened up, and he could no longer breathe. The room had filled with poisonous gas.

A short time later, his heart stopped beating.

CHAPTER SEVENTEEN
SAMUEL

There was an instant after Booger's heart stopped that his memories went back to the bridge that led to the City. The detective had almost died not that long ago, and he had struggled to remember the details of his near-death experience. What he knew for sure was that if he fully crossed the bridge, his life on Earth would be over, and there would be no going back to Rose. He couldn't stand to leave her alone, so he stopped himself and chose to go back to her. Now, the memories of that experience were flooding back. The details of his brief time on the other side were suddenly crystal clear.

He had taken a deep breath. He stepped forward. His family, all his loved ones from the past, were waiting for him just a few feet away. Nancy, his first wife, was there, smiling and with her arms out to greet him. The last time he saw her alive, in the hospital room, her body ravaged with cancer. She was so thin and weak. But the Nancy in front of him was young, healthy, and beautiful. She was exactly the way he remembered her on their Wedding Day. His parents, his brother, grandparents, aunts, and uncles all looked exactly as he remembered them when he was a young boy. No one looked the way they did in the days and months leading up to their death. They looked exactly the way Booger wanted them to look, the way they appeared in his fondest memories of them.

It would be so easy for him to take those few steps to join them in the City. That was when he saw Samuel, the kangaroo man. He was on the left side of Booger, down a short path away from his spiritual home. He wasn't encouraging Booger to come to him. There was no smile. He did not have his arms out waiting to greet him. He gave only a solemn look of understanding. God – aka the Creator, the Boss, the Holy One, the Alpha, and the Omega – chooses to co-create everything with everyone via free will.

So, it was up to Booger to decide whether to cross that bridge. That decision came with a price, however. He knew that by going back to Rose, he might never get an opportunity to live in the City with his loved ones in quite the same way. While all souls would eventually return home – to the City of Gold, also known as heaven – free will ensured that individuals could always choose other options.

As Samuel had told him, *"There is no Hell in the sense that we understand it. Hell is on Earth. In a word, hell is loneliness. Hell is separation from love, just as Earth is separated from Heaven. That's why we grieve when someone we love dies – because we are separated from them. That is where free will gives us the opportunity to live a good, just life, but also to make the wrong choices that lead to a Hellish experience. Throughout life, there are forks in the road. One leading in the right direction, where we will have no regrets about that decision, and one leading in the wrong direction, where there will be regrets. These forks in the road are not easily identified, and the decision to take one path or another is rarely clear."*

Booger had the choice to stay dead. He could have enjoyed his time in the place where all are loved and all belong, and waited to welcome Rose to the City when her time was up. But Rose needed her husband. She begged for Booger to come back, to not leave her, and so that's what he did.

Samuel knew all about how such choices could be complicated. He was a fallen angel. Eons ago, he created his own distinctive kangaroo tail as a symbol of his unique abilities. Samuel, the angel of worlds, routinely hopped between parallel realities. It was who he was.

Samuel was among the first angels born into God's kingdom. The group, known as the 8 because there were eight of them, grew up together and built the City as the eternal home for all of creation. Each angel had their own talents, but in those early days, their gifts were not specialized. Those came about organically through their own free will. As their interests grew, so did their abilities. For example, the angel Thaddeus became enamored with mathematics, while the angel Marie was fascinated with physics. Collectively, their talents grew to fit with each other's abilities like puzzle pieces, and so it was under the collaboration of the 8 that the great City of Gold was built.

Because Samuel was the youngest of the angels and the last to be born, his section to develop was naturally on the periphery of the City. As he built the gates, he began to notice that in looking beyond them, his mind was creating a landscape. Features were being born into the void just through his imagination. In time, he became more and more infatuated with the idea of creating worlds beyond the gates, which was not an interest that he shared with any other angels. They were all busy creating a paradise for themselves and the future of the Boss' creation.

Eventually, Samuel spoke to God and told him that he thought there were an infinite number of worlds he could create beyond the gates, but he'd need to leave the City to do so. God told Samuel that he could go beyond the gates, but that if he did, he'd create a way for other spirits to leave the safe haven of paradise, too.

"*My will is your will,*" the Boss said. "*But when you do what you do, you must become a shepherd to all those who follow you. The City was designed by the 8 to be a home for all of creation for all time, so when my children want to explore your worlds, they must be available to help bring them home. This is your choice, but it's also your responsibility.*"

And so Samuel ventured beyond the gates. Over the next 1000 hours, the eighth angel created 1000 worlds within his first universe, which was as big as his mind could imagine. This act of creation made him feel deeply fulfilled. And, over time, he'd create many more and would jump back and forth between them with ease. But he didn't want to create everything just for himself. Other angels could leave the City and visit Samuel's worlds, but they seldom did. So, eventually, God created the spirits that would become man and woman to fill Samuel's world, called Earth. Their purpose was the same as any other creature – to be themselves fully and enjoy God's creation. And, bit by bit, people brought pieces of heaven down with them to enrich the world through ideas, such as Thaddeus' mathematics. Once Samuel realized he had people to live in and explore his worlds, he began to lure them one by one beyond the gates. But luring people beyond their natural spiritual home came with a price. It meant that as long as there were people exploring his creation, he needed to live outside of the City. And as long as he was outside of the City, he was largely cut off from his angelic family.

So, there was an inherent sacrifice built into his creation. In choosing to devote his time to his worlds, he was also choosing to be away from his home and those he loved most. Outside of the gates, he became the greatest of all creators, the most accomplished of angels, but this path made him lonely. And so, a paradox emerged. Samuel needed new spirits to fill his universe and to keep him company, and to fulfill his spirit through the gifts he had developed, but drawing them outside the gates kept him away from his home.

"*This is the reason for the duality of our world,*" Samuel told Booger. "*I am filled with love for all of creation, but I am sad because I am so near home, yet it's always just beyond my reach.*"

In that same way, every soul who ventures outside the gates of the City feels lost to some degree. That's because there is loneliness built into everything. It's this deep-seated sadness that causes souls to turn against God, to turn against people, to be selfish, and to turn against oneself. Because of this, often, when souls return home, they don't stay long. Once in the presence of unconditional love, they feel shame for how they acted when they were away. They want to go back to Earth or other worlds, to be reincarnated, to do a better job of serving others and extending love beyond the gates.

With Booger's heart momentarily stopped, he remembered it all. He knew what he'd so easily forgotten. That's when he saw Samuel again.

"It's a little soon for you to be getting yourself killed again, don't you think?"

"Yeah, well, that wasn't my intention," Booger said, now feeling like he was speaking to an old friend.

"I know your intentions, and it's not your time. I can't save you from your choices, but I will help you when you need help most," Samuel said as he snapped his fingers, and Booger's heart instantly started beating again.

When the detective suddenly jolted back to life, he gasped for air and then found that one of the shackles that was holding him upright to the wall had come loose. Booger then was able to reach for his trusty friend and wiggle the other shackle, unlocking it before he fell to the floor. When he lifted his body, Samuel was gone, and the door to the room was open.

Booger stopped briefly, pulled out his cell phone, and took pictures of both rooms, the shackles, the beds, the table with torture tools, everything. The police might not believe what he saw, but they'd have to believe the pictures, he thought.

He carefully opened the door to the torture room and walked into the tunnel. He wasn't certain in what direction he needed to go to escape. *"Were his captors in the inn, or had they gone back to the drug lab or maybe to the Landers Theatre?"*

In his mind's eye, Booger sensed that Samuel was pointing him back to the Landers Theatre even though the inn was much closer, and all he wanted was to escape this tunnel as fast as possible.

The detective stopped briefly at the other door, the one that Brandon had said was a drug lab. He could hear the muffled sounds of people inside. But he wasn't going to chance trying to get a look. Instead, he continued down the tunnel. Soon, he reached the point where the tunnel narrowed and became lower. He bent his head and continued on. The fresh oxygen ended and was replaced with air vents every so often. When the lights and the tunnel turned dark, Booger slowed down and used the wall as a guide. He had lost his flashlight in the basement of the inn, and the darkness blinded him.

It was a long, slow road, but he didn't run into anyone, which meant he would live. He had made the right choice. By the time he'd gotten to the theater, it was completely dark outside. He climbed up the coal chute to the outside, found his car, and drove off.

He was just about to call Detective Jelks when his cell phone rang. It was the detective calling him.

"Booger McClain, I need to talk to you."

"Great timing, Jelks. I was just about to call you. I can be at your office in about ten minutes."

"No, McClain. I don't want to meet you here. How about someplace else?"

"Well, I could use a drink, Jelks. How about Big Curly's Bar in, say, 20 minutes?"

"OK, see you there."

CHAPTER EIGHTEEN
DETECTIVE WALTER JELKS

It was karaoke night at Big Curly's, and the place was nearly packed. Booger managed to find a table in a corner away from the stage and much of the noise. He sat down and ordered two Pabst beers and two shots of whisky.

The barmaid, Janene, a woman in her forties wearing a sheer V-neck blouse, two sizes too small, and wearing heavy makeup, looked at Booger with a smile, "You're wanting to get drunk fast. Aren't you, cowboy?"

"The faster, the better."

Just a couple of minutes later, Walter Jelks walked in. Booger motioned to him, and he came over and sat down. "I hope you didn't order me anything, McClain. I'm still on duty."

"Nope. I just ordered for me.

Janene walked over to the table holding drinks and put one of the beers, and shot down in front of Booger and the other in front of Jelks.

"I thought you said that you didn't order me a drink, McClain," Jelks said, staring at the drinks in front of him.

"I didn't," Booger said, reaching over and moving the drinks to his side of the table.

Janene looked Jelks over before asking, "You a cop?"

"Yes."

"I thought so. Drinks are on the house if you want

something."

"No. I'm fine."

Booger reached up and touched Janene's arm. "I'm a cop too."

"No, you're not."

"How can you tell?"

"Well, for one, you're not wearing a tie that has food stains on it, and two, because your clothes are dirty, and you smell like you've been in a sewer."

"Janene, I like you," Booger said, smiling back.

"OK, McClain. First, why don't you tell me what you want to talk to me about, and then we'll get to why I called you."

"I discovered a connection between Landers Theatre and the Walnut Street Inn."

"What is it?"

"A tunnel."

"McClain, were you drinking before I got here?"

"Yes, but only a sip or two."

"Well, you're not making any sense."

"There's a tunnel that runs between the Landers Theatre and The Walnut Street Inn."

"Yeah, I know about it."

"What?"

"Yeah, there's a tunnel that was built a hundred years ago during the bootlegging days when drinking was prohibited. The tunnel runs underneath or alongside a number of bars and businesses and was used to hide and deliver booze during the time of prohibition. It's no secret, McClain."

"Well, that tunnel has been modernized, and it's now used for human trafficking and to produce cocaine."

"And what evidence do you have?"

"I've been inside, and I've got pictures on my cell phone," Booger said, handing his phone over to the detective. Brandon Landers tried to kill me, and I'm sure he was responsible for the death of Cornilus Landers and probably Bob Williams."

"Have you shown these pictures to anyone else?"

"No, just you."

"Well, don't. Particularly, not the police."

"Why?"

"Because I think several are on the Landers payroll."

"Who?"

"I don't know yet, but I intend to find out."

"What about Brandon Landers?"

"McClain, you're not telling me anything that I don't already know. At least I know that he was likely responsible for the death of Cornilus."

"Then, for God's sake, why is my wife in jail for suspicion of his murder?"

"That's why I called you, McClain. The D.A. is probably going to release her in the morning. We found poison in Cornilus' bloodstream. He was dead before your wife shot him. As for Bob Williams, your wife didn't shoot him either. The bullet the medical examiner pulled out, the one that killed Williams, came from a 9mm Glock. Your wife's gun was used to fire a bullet into him, but it was after he was already dead."

"A Glock, huh? The same gun that is standard issue for the Springfield police?"

"Yes, but don't jump to conclusions, McClain. Plenty of other people own Glocks."

"So, Jelks, is that why you didn't want to meet me at the police station?"

"Yes, but it's just a precaution. We don't know for certain

that an officer is involved."

"But you're confident Rose wasn't involved now?"

"Yes."

"Can I pick Rose up in the morning?"

"Yes."

"Jelks, there is something else in the basement of the Walnut Street Inn."

"What?"

"Bodies, I think. At least it looks like graves have been dug down there."

"Shit."

"Jelks, what are you going to do about the tunnel?"

"First, I'll need to get a search warrant. Then I'll go take a look."

"By yourself?"

"No. There are a few officers I can trust. I'll bring them with me. But I don't want to get anyone else involved yet–not until I know what is there and who, if anyone, from the police department is involved."

"Jelks, I'd like to go with you. I can show you where everything is."

"OK, McClain. I think you would be helpful. But no gun, and stay out of our way. Let's plan on going tomorrow at dusk. You can meet me outside the Walnut Street Inn."

"That sounds like a plan."

Walter Jelks had a reputation for solving cases. He was hard-nosed and detail-oriented.

The detective had been married to his high school sweetheart for the last few years. He connected with her on social media after his third divorce. They had no children. Mary Jelks was thirty-seven when she was diagnosed with cancer of the uterus. She underwent a hysterectomy, and children were no longer an option.

Recently, the cancer returned. She had undergone radiation therapy and two operations. Nothing had been successful, and now she was in hospice care. The bills were mounting, and so was the stress on her husband. Though no one was aware of it. Walter Jelks was an old-school man. He kept his personal troubles to himself. Only a handful of people even knew his wife's cancer had returned, and no one knew how serious her condition was.

Every morning before work and every night after work, he spent time at his wife's bedside. Not long ago, he had hope. The John Hopkins Hospital had a very good success rate with getting her kind of cancer into remission. But his insurance wouldn't cover it, and the cost was beyond his means. Now, it was too late. Each day, he prayed for a miracle, and each day, she faded further away.

After leaving the bar, Walter Jelks drove to Andy's and got a BootDaddy concrete. It was his wife's favorite. They had shared one on their first date. Then he drove to Brookhaven, the long-term care facility where Mary had spent the last three months of her life.

As he walked in the front door to the lobby, Carol Lister saw him enter and asked to speak with him briefly. Carol was the administrator of the facility.

"Detective Jelks, may I please have a quick word with you?"

"How about on the way out, Ms. Lister? I brought Mary some ice cream, and I don't want it to melt."

"This will only take a minute, detective."

"Ok, but please make it quick."

"Detective, it's about your wife's bill. We haven't received a payment from you in nearly two months. As you might imagine, hospice care requires around-the-clock care for your wife, and it is rather expensive."

"Yes, I understand, Ms. Lister, and I should have payment for you in two to three days."

"You know, detective, your wife's condition is, well, not very good. She doesn't really know what is going on around her. What I'm getting at, detective, is that there are Medicare beds available at several facilities that would cost substantially less than Brookhaven."

"Let me stop you right there, Ms. Lister," Walter Jelks said in a forceful voice. "I chose Brookhaven for my wife because it's the best, and my wife deserves the best. Now I told you that I'll have the money in a few days. So, please let me go visit my wife."

"Yes, detective."

Walter Jelks went down the hallway to the last room on the right, opened it, and walked in. The lights were out except for one soft light on the nightstand next to his wife.

Mary was lying on her back with her mouth open, sound asleep.

He walked to her side and just looked at her for several seconds. She was not the vivacious woman he had known years earlier. The cancer had ravaged her. Now she was so thin, her bones showed through her skin. Her face was thin and worn. But lying in her bed asleep, she was beautiful. She was just like an angel, and she was his whole world.

Walter Jelks leaned over and kissed his wife on the cheek. For a second, she opened her eyes and looked at him. He recognized his beloved Mary in her eyes. Those soft blue eyes were just as they'd always been. They showed the love and strength that he remembered.

"Hi, honey. I brought you a BootDaddy from Andy's.

She forced a brief smile and then closed her eyes again. He called a nurse and asked her to put the concrete in the freezer and give it to his wife when she was awake.

"You know it's useless, detective. She won't eat anything now. We've got to feed her through IVs."

"Please, nurse, just put it in the freezer, and I'll try again in the morning."

CHAPTER NINETEEN
ROSE GETS OUT OF JAIL

Booger arrived at the jail early the next morning. But it was nearly three hours before the order to release his wife came through, and then they had to process her.

At nearly 11 am, Rose walked out of the jail into her husband's arms. "Booger McClain, I am so glad to see you," she said, hugging him with all her strength.

"I missed you, too, sweetie. How was your stay?"

"Fine, if you mind sleeping on a rock-hard bed in a six-by-eight cell with an open toilet and no window."

"Can't be much worse than some of the cabins we've stayed in."

"True."

"How about the food?"

"Powdered eggs, stale bread, and peanut butter."

"Well, how about a good, home-cooked meal?"

"Buford, you don't cook."

"I know. I was thinking about a McDonalds home-cooked meal."

"Sounds good to me."

Booger held his wife's hand and walked her to his red Corvette, parked just outside. He opened the door for her and gave her a kiss on the cheek.

Rose knew her husband loved her, but she didn't know

how much he missed her until he opened that car door for her. Booger was a macho guy and certainly not one for showing his love in public. She couldn't remember the last time he held her hand in public, nor could she remember the last time he opened the car door for her. Rose had never minded. She knew that expressing emotions and displaying affection when others could see was out of character for him. Besides, her husband was plenty affectionate when they were alone, and she had never questioned his love for her.

Inside the car, Booger put the top down and reached for the glove compartment to pull a bright purple scarf out. He handed it to his wife and smiled. It was a thoughtful gesture. Whenever the top on Booger's car was down, Rose wore a scarf to keep her hair from getting messed up. His wife noted that it wouldn't have mattered that day because her hair was a mess from spending a couple of days in jail. But she appreciated the gesture just as well.

As she wrapped her hair in the scarf, she looked up at the sky and said, "Sweetie, did you notice the dark clouds just to our west?"

"Yeah, but the weatherman said there was no chance of rain today."

"OK, dear."

Booger started the car, turned the radio station to 94.7 KTTS Country, and drove off to the closest McDonalds.

Five minutes later and two blocks from McDonalds, the dark clouds had moved directly overhead, and just as he pulled into the parking lot, it began to downpour. People seated in the restaurant had their eyes glued to Booger and Rose as he desperately tried to get the top up on the car with one hand while holding his white Stetson cowboy hat over his wife's head with the other. Rose just smiled. A few seconds later, the radio announcer said, "My, my, the weatherman certainly got today wrong, folks." Then he played "Rain is a Good Thing" by Luke Bryant. Rose's smile turned to laughter.

"Two Big Mac value meals with coffee and a change of clothes, please," Booger yelled into the speaker when the worker asked for his order.

When Booger was served the bag of food, Rose grabbed it from him and devoured her Big Mac and fries within minutes of leaving the drive-thru.

"Sweetie, I've never seen you eat that fast," Booger replied.

"Well, I never thought McDonalds could taste this good, but after eating powdered eggs and stale bread for a few days, this was fantastic. Do you mind if I have some of your fries, Booger?"

"No, just leave a few crumbs for me."

"Booger, the district attorney said the charges against me in the Landers' murder were dropped. But he didn't say why. Have you learned anything new? Do you know who killed Cornilus Landers?"

"I'd guess it was his brother and sister. They stood to gain the most from his death. Not just the Landers Theatre, but the money from drugs and human trafficking."

"OK, dear. I guess you need to catch me up on what's happened."

As Rose wolfed down the remainder of her husband's fries, Booger told his wife about the tunnel, the two rooms, and the graves in the basement.

"Oh my. So do you think that's why Bob Williams was murdered?"

"Yes, I think he had a change of heart over what was going on underneath the Bed & Breakfast. I'd guess that Cornilus murdered him. Then Brandon and maybe Ida murdered Cornilus. It was all because of greed. Just before he tried to kill me…"

"What?"

"Sweetie, I need to give you the condensed version of what's going on. Brandon and Pat tried to kill me. In fact, you could say they succeeded, but then Samuel appeared and saved me."

"Samuel?"

"Yes, from up above. You know, the kangaroo man."

"Oh, yes. Things are so much clearer now. Maybe I need the condensed, condensed version."

"OK. Drugs, human trafficking, dead bodies, Brandon, Ida, Pat, and Sue are involved."

"See, that wasn't so hard, was it, dear?"

"No. And so you understand everything now, Rose?"

"No. But I trust you do. So, how can I help?"

"You can stay home and rest. You've been through enough. I've got everything under control."

"You and the kangaroo man that I've never seen."

"Yes, that's right."

"Booger McClain, either you've lost all your marbles, or you're seeing things that don't exist. Either way, I'm going with you wherever you go. You need my help even if you are too stubborn to admit it."

"Now that's the woman I love," Booger said, leaning over and giving his wife a kiss on the cheek.

CHAPTER TWENTY
THE DEVIL AFTER MIDNIGHT

It was 2 am when Randolph walked out of the inn to the passenger van, where he covered the name on the side of the bed-and-breakfast's van with a magnetic sign that read, "Helping Hands Ministry." Then he got into the passenger van and drove away. It was a cold evening, and dressed in a winter coat and gloves, he was shivering when he turned the van's heater on high. It would take several minutes for the heater to be effective, so he turned the radio to a Christian radio channel in hopes it would distract him from the chill running through his bones. He was not particularly fond of Christian music, but that was the music his passengers would expect to hear.

Randolph was on a mission, one he had done many times in the past. He glanced in the rear-view mirror at the ten-passenger seats behind him. He had been instructed to pick up ten guests. If his mission was successful, the van would be completely full in an hour or so.

The thin, young man had worked at the Walnut Street Inn for nearly two years. Mostly, he worked at the front desk, but during slow times, he did whatever his boss told him to do. The job barely paid a livable wage, but in Springfield, that was more common than not. Besides, he was a drug addict, and finding work was difficult. It was these late-night passenger pick-ups that would feed his cocaine habit. The Landers' siblings were well aware of his drug addiction, and they used that to coerce him into making these late-night pick-ups. He needed his drugs, and Cornilus and Brandon Landers provided those drugs every time he made a successful pick-up.

Randolph was a fully functioning junkie. He was a unique person who could be high, and he was most of the time, and still functioned like a sober person. Brandon had discovered him on the streets two years earlier when the Landers' kid was making a pick-up. Brandon couldn't tell he was a junkie, and he was one of the ten people Brandon picked up that night. His addiction was discovered during a more thorough examination at the inn. Cornilus considered disposing of him in a grave in the basement, but Brandon was insistent that his unique quality of looking and acting sober even when he was high meant he could be put to good use. They could get cheap labor that would be dependent on them and willing to do whatever they asked. By feeding his cocaine habit, they would have a very loyal employee, one who would look the other way when need be. Randolph became an excellent employee willing to perform any task his bosses wanted. He was likeable, trustworthy, and diligent, but most of all, he kept secrets.

Sundays were his pick-up nights. The streets were nearly empty after 10 pm, and it was prime time to search for guests without others watching. Their stay would be for a week, and on the following Sunday, they would depart for St. Louis.

The streets of Springfield were nearly empty at that time of morning. Springfield was a family town, early to bed, early to rise, hardworking, God-fearing, salt of the earth type of people. People who were exhausted from Church that day and partying the night before. Monday was a workday, so Sunday night was a time to go to bed early. It was a Christian town that hid its dark underbelly very well.

Randolph drove slowly from the southern edge of the city through downtown and finally to the northwest side of Springfield, where the least fortunate and most needy lived. This was where he would find his ten guests. He went down a dimly lit Commercial Street with seedy bars where scantily dressed women in high heels and short skirts roamed the street looking for a date. Even the police avoided this section of town unless they were called there.

Randolph counted on that. In these neighborhoods, police weren't a presence, and people tended to keep to themselves. His dark-colored extended van slowly roaming the streets north of Chestnut Expressway in the middle of the night would hardly be noticed and, even if it was, would be forgotten the next day.

These were the streets of forgotten, invisible, and unwanted souls. Their lives were not top of mind to most of the good citizens of Springfield, and Randolph knew that the ten souls he found tonight would not be missed.

He looked over the ladies of the night as he drove slowly down one block, then another. He had visited them many times, in a different car, to ask for a date. This, too, was encouraged by Cornilus. But he had never considered one a guest he would bring back to the inn. The Landers siblings were very particular about their guests. "No one on drugs, only young, strong, healthy people," Cornilus had told him before. "Our clients demand the best, and that's what we provide them."

In an alleyway behind a dive bar named Dave's, south of Division, he saw a small group of homeless people gathered. They blended into the night with only the occasional striking of a match or burning of newspaper in a trash barrel to keep warm, being the only way to distinguish them from the darkness surrounding them.

This was an area where a slow-moving van with a "Helping Hands Ministry" sign on its side got attention. When he stopped in the alleyway, the homeless came out of the darkness in anticipation of Christian kindness.

These lost souls were in desperate need of help. A meal, a warm and safe place to spend the night, a blanket, anything that would make life a little less harsh for them, even if it was only for the night.

When an ample number of lost souls had gathered around the van, Randolph got out and looked them over. "Folks, Helping Hands has room to provide a meal, bath, clothes, and a room for the night for ten God-fearing Christians. No drugs, no alcohol. You must be sober and willing to listen to the word of the Lord."

He moved throughout the crowd, looking for the young and healthy amongst them. When he found one, Randolph would examine their arms for needle marks, smell their breath for alcohol, and look into their eyes for any sign of addiction. If they passed the requirements he was given, he would open the van door for them. He duplicated the same process ten times, and when the van was full, he drove off.

It was after 3 am. Randolph drove through the quiet streets of Springfield to the Walnut Street Inn. Waiting inside the lobby for him and the guests were Brandon and Ida Landers, and Pat and Cindy Williams. They greeted each guest with enthusiastic smiles while examining each one for signs of drug or alcohol addiction.

Then, as promised, each was ushered into the dining room for a home-cooked meal of pot roast in thick brown gravy, potatoes, carrots, biscuits and honey, and apple pie for dessert.

After dinner, each guest was assigned a room and

encouraged to take a shower. Pajamas and a new set of clothes were waiting for them in the rooms.

Just before the lights were turned off, each room was locked from the outside to prevent any chance of escape during the night.

When asked about that by several of the guests, the response was, "It's so as not to disturb any of the other guests by wandering through the inn late at night."

Fed until they were full, content that another meal would be coming in the morning, and in a clean bedroom, there was never any objection from the guests.

"Wear your new clothes to breakfast in the morning," Pat and Brandon would say. "After breakfast, there will be a short prayer service, and then you will be taken back to the streets with a new winter coat and a blanket.

At 9 am, the doors would be unlocked, and men would be waiting in the hallways for each guest to come out of their room wearing their new clothes. Then, they were led downstairs to breakfast. Coffee, juice, bacon, scrambled eggs, and hashbrowns with a generous dose of succinylcholine powder mixed inside the coffee, juice, and scrambled eggs.

Five minutes later, paralysis began. Not long after, none of the guests could move. They were all in a state of conscious sedation. Sue's job as a surgical nurse provided her access to the very effective drug.

Completely immobilized, the guests were carried down to the basement, then into the tunnel, and finally to the room with beds that had leg and arm restraints. This would be their home for the next seven days.

In that room, the cooperative would be fed and taken care of, and the uncooperative would be tortured and starved until they were silenced.

Although most guests would eventually become cooperative, once in a while, someone would not conform. Those were the souls that were buried in the basement of the inn.

Normally, by the following Sunday, the guests were successfully indoctrinated and ready to be transported to their final home.

That's when the guests would receive their second dose of the paralytic drug and be loaded into an unmarked white cargo van driven by Pat Williams to a warehouse on the South side of St. Louis. There, they would be kept in a paralytic state while transportation was arranged to deliver the guests to the clients who purchased the free labor. Most went to gold mining clients in South America, but some were delivered into sex trafficking rings from all over the world. All would be sent to foreign countries. Payment was made in cash and was always COD.

CHAPTER TWENTY-ONE
DANGEROUS ENCOUNTER

Booger's cell phone rang at a few minutes past 11 pm that night.

"McClain, this is Jelks. Meet me in the parking lot across the street from the Landers Theatre at 2 am sharp."

"Jelks, you're not much on niceties or small talk, are you?"

"Be there at exactly 2 am, not a minute late."

"OK, by the way, I'm bringing Rose."

"You're putting your wife in danger. I wouldn't do that if I were you."

"Have you met Rose, detective?" My life is in more danger if I don't bring her."

"Fine, 2 am sharp."

"Roger that, detective."

It was 1:45 am when the McClains got in Booger's red Corvette and headed to the parking lot across from the Landers Theatre.

"Do you have your gun with you?" Booger asked his wife.

"I never leave home without it."

"That's my girl."

"How many police are going to be there?"

"I don't know, not many, I think. Jelks said that he wasn't sure who he could trust, so he's going to be careful about who he brings."

"So, I trust the police department doesn't know about this

operation?"

"A few of them do. Jelks had to go to a judge to get a warrant to enter both businesses. So, I figure he had to tell his boss, plus the detectives, he's brought with him tonight."

"Well, let's hope we can all trust the people he told and the ones he's bringing with him. Otherwise, we're going to be in a world of hurt."

A block from the Landers Theatre, Booger turned the headlights off. At 1:57 am, he pulled into the parking lot across the street. One lone car was parked in the very back of the lot.

The red Corvette pulled up next to the car. "Stay here, Rose. Let me talk to Jelks first."

Booger opened the passenger door to Jelk's tan Chevy and sat down next to the detective."

"When's the cavalry coming?" Booger asked.

"What?"

"The cavalry."

"I don't know what you're talking about."

"Jelks, don't tell me you haven't heard the term, 'when's the cavalry coming?'"

"No, I haven't, McClain."

"Well, in this context, it means, when are the other police coming?"

"They aren't."

"What?"

"They aren't coming here to the Landers Theatre. I've got two men I trust that will converge on the Walnut Street Inn at the same time we enter the Landers. That way, no one will be able to escape without going through us."

"Brilliant, Jelks. You do remember that I told you there are likely dozens of them in there?"

"Yeah."

"And you think the five of us can stop them?"

"Yeah."

"Damn, Jelks. Rose and I may as well leave now. Did you ever hear of Custer's last stand or the Alamo? Those guys were outnumbered by less than we will be."

"Do as you please, McClain. I'm going in whether you're with me or not."

"Crap, Jelks. You know I can't let you go alone."

The two men got out of the car, as did Rose. Booger turned to his wife and said, "Listen, sweetie, change of plans. I need you to stay in the car and keep a lookout for anyone who might escape."

"No way, old man. I'm going in with you."

"Rose, please, can't you just do what I say?" Booger said in an angry voice.

Rose glared at her husband with a shocked look. Booger had never made a comment like that before and certainly had never been that cross with her. Then she saw the look on her husband's face. His face was begging her not to come along. She instantly knew that something was terribly wrong.

"OK," she said. "I'll wait in the car."

With that, the two men walked away, across the street and toward the back of the theatre. Rose waited a few minutes until they had disappeared out of sight, then she walked toward the theater. There was no way that she was going to sit in that car, knowing that her husband was in trouble. She would follow them inside and just try to keep her distance. Rose would be there in case her husband needed her.

Booger walked Jelks toward the old coal shaft, which he had used before to enter the Landers Theatre undetected.

Just as it came into sight, the two detectives heard the sound of a large vehicle coming in their direction. The headlights were off, so it was impossible to see what it was until it got close.

McClain and Jelks fell to the ground behind some overgrown bushes next to the side of the building.

They watched as a school bus with the side marked "College of the Ozarks" drove past them. It stopped next to the coal chute and then backed in to within ten feet of the chute. Within seconds, a dozen or so men came out of the coal chute. Several were carrying some sort of pulley. The others climbed into the exit door of the school bus.

McClain and Jelks moved closer to get a better look. Forty feet from the action, they got a good look at the men with the pulley as they hoisted pallet after pallet, each stacked three feet high with hundreds of small plastic-wrapped items.

"Cocaine?" Booger whispered to Jelks.

"Could be," he whispered back.

The activity on the school bus was obscured from their vision. But soon, men began loading the white powdery substance onto the school bus. The detectives watched as the men appeared to be loading the plastic-wrapped items one by one in an area underneath the floor of the vehicle.

"A false bottom," Booger whispered.

"Yes," Jelks replied.

When everything on the pallets was loaded, the bus drove off, and the men went back into the theatre through a rear door.

Booger got on his cell phone to ask his wife to follow the bus. But the call went to voicemail. "Shit," Booger responded. He didn't know for sure, but his gut feeling said that either his wife had been captured or she had ignored his request and had left the car to follow him.

Booger speculated that the trafficking part of the Inn's business made hundreds of thousands of dollars for the Landers family every year. But it was tiny in comparison to the money made from the drug lab.

"If that is cocaine that they loaded on the bus," Booger said to Jelks, "It must have a street value of $20-30 million dollars."

Then he cautioned Jelks, "You need to get back up, lots of backup."

"I told you, McClain, I can't trust calling this in. We need to do this ourselves."

After a couple of minutes, Jelks turned to Booger and said, "It's time to go."

The Springfield detective led the way down the coal chute and into the basement of the Landers Theatre. Booger followed closely behind.

The coal chute was not Booger's preferred option for getting into the building. His large, framed body shot down the chute at a fast rate, creating friction to his backside that felt like fire radiating from his body. And as painful as the trip down the chute was for him, it paled in comparison to the pain of landing on a concrete floor.

"You want help up, old man?" Jelks asked with a smile.

"No, I'm fine," he replied, trying to hide the pained look on his face.

Booger got to his feet and tried one more time to call Rose. She did not answer. "OK, let's get going," McClain said to Jelks.

As much as it pained him to do, sliding down that coal chute was the fastest way to the tunnel. He landed in one corner of the basement, and the tunnel was a hundred yards or so on the other side of the basement. It would be easier to get to the tunnel this time. Unlike before, the lights were on in the basement.

"Where do you suppose the officers you brought with you are now, Jelks?"

"Securing the Bed & Breakfast so no one can get out that way."

"So, it's just you and me to encounter the bad guys?"

"Yes."

"Those aren't good odds, Jelks."

"No, they're not."

"Why not call for backup now? We're in the building, and so are the officers you brought with you. Even if they are alerted that the police are coming, we are on both ends of the tunnel and should be able to stop them or at least slow them down until the cavalry gets here."

"Later, McClain. I'll call them, but not yet."

"Then when?"

"When we're in the tunnel and are certain the bad guys are there."

"Well, can you at least call the officers you brought with you to see if they've come across anybody?"

"Damn, McClain, be patient. I was just about to do that."

Jelks pulled out his cell phone and dialed. "Johnson, where are you?"

"We're outside the inn. There are quite a few people being carried out of the building and loaded into a van. They appear to be incapacitated."

"Johnson, you were supposed to go inside."

"The place has a lot of activity coming and going. I didn't want to tip them off that we're coming."

"Well, in ten minutes, I need you inside. Subdue whoever is in the inn and move down to the basement."

"Yeah, yeah, okay."

"That van, Jelks. I think they are loading people that they picked up on the streets into it and driving them out of town."

"Could be, McClain."

"Shouldn't you alert the police so they can follow that van?"

"Not yet, McClain. I don't want to tip anyone off until we get closer."

Booger shook his head in disgust. It just didn't make any sense not to call for backup now. Jelks either had a death wish or he had a hero complex. The two detectives began walking. They moved quietly in and out of the rows of shelving, trying to stay hidden in case some bad guys were in the basement.

Every so often, they would hear a noise and stop. Mostly, the noises came from the large furnace or from the creaks of a hundred-year-old building. But on two occasions, they heard distant voices. When they did, the detectives would stop and try to determine where the voices were coming from. That wasn't easy, considering the natural echoes that came from the basement and the tunnel they were approaching.

Only when Jelks determined the voices were too far away to be dangerous would the two detectives continue.

Seeing the basement in the light gave Booger a new perspective on its enormity. There were thousands of items, big and small, housed down there. There were at least fifteen rows of shelves. Each row contained thirty feet of shelving on both sides, stacked from the floor to about two feet from the ceiling, approximately eight feet high. Seasonal props, clothing, and decorations. There appeared to be little organization, with one exception. The final row contained the macabre designs. Freaks, demons, ghosts, Halloween nightmares. Creatures of every size, all frightening and terribly realistic. If the Landers Theatre was actually haunted, these would be the creatures doing it. Walking through that aisle gave Booger chills, although it didn't seem to bother Walker Jelks.

Past that aisle and down a walkway was the wall that contained the tunnel entrance. When they arrived there, the detectives stopped for a minute to listen for any voices. There were no sounds. Before entering, Jelks called Johnson again to confirm that his team had entered the Walnut Street Inn. But the call went unanswered.

McClain had a sick feeling in his stomach. Something was wrong. He knew it. "Call for backups, Jelks."

"OK," Jelks replied as he got on his cell phone. "Break-in at Landers Theatre. Officers in trouble inside a tunnel in the basement of the theatre, extending to the basement of the Walnut Street Inn. Approach from both sides with caution."

Seconds after making the call, the detectives opened the door leading into the tunnel. It was pitch black inside, and both men pulled out flashlights and shot the beams of light straight ahead. Then they started walking through the narrow openings where they were forced to bend over as they walked to get through the tight spaces. "How long is it like this, McClain?" Jelks asked. "My back's killing me."

"Not long, detective, just a few minutes of walking."

Not far into the tunnel, breathing became more labored. "Something's wrong, Jelks. We're not getting any fresh air."

Another hundred feet, the men reached an air vent in the ceiling. Booger put the palm of his hand over the opening. "There is no air coming through. Someone has closed the vents. Damn Jelks. They must know we're coming."

"I don't know how they would know, McClain."

"All I know is that the air is going to get very thin soon. I think we should turn back Jelks and wait for backup."

"McClain, you're a wimp. We've come too far to turn back now."

CHAPTER TWENTY-TWO
ROSE TO THE RESCUE

Rose McClain waited in the car across from the Landers Theatre until her husband and the detective were out of sight. She was never one for sitting on the bench while others played the game. Besides, her husband needed her, whether he would admit it or not.

So, Rose got out of Booger's red Corvette and walked across the street and to the side of the building, following the direction Booger had gone. She placed her cell phone on vibrate so it wouldn't ring and give away her position.

The app she had recently purchased and put on Booger's cell phone to track it had paid off. It did not provide his exact position, but it got close, and she began following it.

Rose saw a school bus approach the Landers, and just before it got to the parking lot, it turned its headlights off. She moved quickly to the shrubbery next to the building and crouched down so as not to be seen by the driver. The bus drove past her, not more than ten feet away.

When the bus was out of sight, Rose continued her walk along the side of the building. Soon, she noticed that Booger's cell phone had stopped moving, so she stopped, too. The last thing she wanted was to catch up to her husband, at least not now. Rose would remain close but not too close, and she would be there to protect her husband if she needed to.

Soon, she saw a short movement of Booger's cell phone, then it stopped again. The cell phone remained in one spot for what felt like an hour. This made her think that either he left the cell phone there or turned it off.

Then she saw the school bus approaching again from ahead of her. Its lights were turned off, and she hid behind a bush, watching as it went past her. The College of the Ozarks logo was plastered on its side.

When the bus reached the street, the headlights came on as it turned East and headed out of sight. That's when she felt the vibration of her cell phone. It was her husband. She chose not to answer it.

Soon, Booger's cell phone began moving again, and so did Rose. She was about forty yards behind her husband as she watched the tracker go inside the Landers Theatre.

Rose knew approximately where Booger had entered the building, but when she reached the area, there was a wooden cellar door obscured by overgrown weeds. The door had a lock on it. If this was the way Booger had entered the building, it was odd that the door was locked from the outside. Regardless, she still had a set of Landers' keys, and after fumbling with them for a few moments, she found the right one.

Rose opened the door and saw what looked like a metal slide going downward. Lights at the bottom told her the slide angled downward about ten to twelve feet before reaching the basement floor. She sat on the edge and pushed herself down, landing on the concrete floor.

After getting up, she began walking into the basement. A large, noisy furnace was to the right of her. Rows of shelving to the left. She followed the tracker on her phone to the left, past rows of shelving holding remnants and oddities of the past. From the large number of items on the floor and on shelves, Rose could only assume that those who ran the theater never threw anything away.

She found an open pathway near the west wall of the basement and parallel to the office where Cornilus Landers was killed and followed it. As she got close to the office, she heard voices inside, so she moved out of sight down the rows of shelving.

When she reached the last row of shelves, she noticed something odd. The shelves in that row were completely empty. There was nothing there. It was odd because all the other ones were completely full. In fact, they were overflowing with items unable to fit on the shelves, sitting on the concrete floor. This was the only bare row.

Just as she got to the end of that row, she heard the door of the office close and a pair of footsteps approaching. She quickly hid inside one of the bottom shelves and waited for the footsteps to go away. As they passed her, Rose noticed two men walking toward the far wall.

She watched as the men reached a door on the wall, opened it, and walked inside. Waiting until the footsteps disappeared, Rose called 911 and reported a shooting in a tunnel underneath the Walnut Street Inn. She left her cell phone on, hoping the police could track her, then walked the twenty yards or so to the door. She put her ear against it, listening for any sound. Convinced the men were not close, she opened the door and walked inside. A short five-foot-long walkway opened to a tunnel. The tunnel was completely dark, and Rose used the light from her cell phone to guide her inside.

Once inside, she tried calling Booger to alert him to the men approaching, but the call went directly to voicemail. At the same time, the tracker on her husband's phone went dark. He had turned off his phone. Rose began walking toward the last position she had on Booger's phone, hoping he wasn't in danger.

The tunnel was narrow and not more than five feet high, but with Rose's small frame, she was able to walk upright, with the narrow light from her cell phone being the only hint to what was ahead. She was not claustrophobic, but the tight spaces and darkness were unsettling. Air thinned, and Rose's breathing was labored, but she continued. Little creatures ran along the dirt floor. But Rose didn't want to know what they were, so she kept her flashlight pointed straight ahead. Every so often, she would walk into a spiderweb or hear a strange noise that sounded like a bird or a bat, but she continued, knowing that her husband was ahead of her and that he would need her.

Booger had a twenty-minute head start, she figured, so she quickened her pace, hoping to make up some time on him.

Booger and the detective struggled with the lack of fresh air. Their labored breathing slowed them down, and several times, they were forced to stop to rest along the way. Both men were overweight and out of shape, but neither would admit it.

Eventually, they made it to the new section of the tunnel, where fresh oxygen poured in. Their breathing soon returned to normal, and they continued the walk toward the door where the drug lab was located.

McClain sensed trouble before it occurred. He was suspicious of Jelks, though he wasn't certain why. Maybe it was the fact that he didn't bring a lot of backups. Booger could understand that if he were certain, he wouldn't encounter a lot of resistance. But Jelks knew better. He had seen a dozen men loading the school bus. He knew there had to be at least that many more inside. It was like being a part of Custer's last stand, only with Custer knowing he would be outnumbered ten to one but still choosing to attack. It just didn't make any sense. And then there was the phone call to the police requesting backup. Booger found it odd that he didn't hear any voices on the other end of the call. And then it was the officers Jelks supposedly brought with him, the ones entering from the Walnut Street Inn. He heard Johnson's voice when the detective called him, but there was something odd about it. Johnson and his men had not even entered yet. They were still waiting outside. What good were they going to be to Jelks or Booger?

At this point, Booger did not trust Jelks, but he was too far into this to turn back now. Still, he wanted to buy some time and slow things down a bit. Booger believed his wife was likely following him. He knew there was no way she had stayed in the car and didn't answer his calls, so he wanted to give her time to get close. He hoped she would have called the police for reinforcement. If so, they would not be far behind her. McClain couldn't shake the feeling he was walking into a trap, but he thought that maybe he could buy enough time for the cavalry to arrive. That was Custer's fatal mistake.

In the battle of Little Bighorn, Custer had underestimated the number of Native American warriors he would encounter. The battle plan that was drawn up was solid. Custer's 7th Cavalry would approach the enemy from the west, while Colonel John Gibbon's troops would approach the enemy's position from the east. They would trap the Indians and prevent their escape. Had Custer stuck to the plan and waited for Colonel John Gibbon's troops, the outcome would have been much better. But Custer had thought the enemy forces were a fraction of what they actually were, and he was convinced that the 210 men of the 7th cavalry could win the battle with or without John Gibbon's help.

The result, of course, was that all 210 men of the 7th Cavalry died that day, including Colonel Custer.

Booger thought about the Battle of the Little Big Horn as he neared the room with the drug lab. McClain would not underestimate his enemy, and he prayed that the police and his wife would arrive in time to help.

As the two men approached the door to the drug lab, Booger noticed the lights were out in the lab. That was alarming to him. He feared that he was walking into an ambush. Then, when Jelks pushed against the door, and it opened, Booger knew he was in trouble.

Both detectives raised their guns and prepared to enter, Jelks first, followed by McClain.

Rose, in much better shape than her husband and aided by her small frame, which allowed her to stand upright as she moved through the narrow tunnel, was only a few minutes behind him as she reached the new section of the tunnel with concrete walls and floor and fresh air.

The lights were on in that part of the tunnel, and Rose turned her flashlight off and put it in her purse, where she traded it for her small-caliber gun.

She took four steps inside and stopped. Rose was surrounded by shadows on the ceiling, both walls, and floor, large, small, oddly shaped shadows. She called out, but no one answered. It was the strangest thing she had ever encountered. No one was there, yet there were dozens of shadows all around her. She had no explanation for what she saw. At first, the weird occurrence frightened her and sent chills down her back. But then a calmness rushed over her, something she couldn't explain either. It was a good feeling, a feeling that everything would be alright, and Rose began walking again. As she did, the shadows followed her.

Jelks and McClain took two steps inside when Booger felt a metal object slam him in the back of the head. He turned quickly to see two men behind him, one holding the butt of a gun. He thought that he must be getting old not to notice two men coming up behind him, and then Booger fell to the floor.

Rose had just turned the corner when she saw the men behind her husband, and she heard the thud of his body falling to the ground. Then she saw two other men coming up fast from the Landers Theatre side of the tunnel, about thirty feet in front of her. *They must be the men she saw in the basement of the Landers,"* she thought.

She was only twenty feet away when the two men pulled out guns and shot the two officers in the back. Rose pointed her gun toward the men and fired five shots. Both men fell to the ground. She ran to her husband lying just inside the room. "Booger, are you alright?"

He didn't answer but nodded his head. The blow to the head had stunned him, but it would take a lot more than that to damage the old man's hard head.

Rose glanced up to see Detective Walter Jelks pointing his service revolver directly at her. Behind him, she saw Brandon and Ida Landers, and Pat Williams, all armed and pointing guns in her direction.

CHAPTER TWENTY-THREE
BATTLE IN THE TUNNEL

Booger lifted his head from the floor. "Jelks, what the hell are you doing?"

"What does it look like, McClain? I'm working for the Landers."

"Why?" Rose asked. "You're a cop."

"You see, McClain, being a policeman in Springfield doesn't pay very much, and well, with my wife's illness, the medical bills were adding up. The Landers kids offered me the opportunity to pay off everything I owed and afford a few of the luxuries in life that I could never earn on a detective first-class salary. All I needed to do was take care of any problems. And McClain, you and your wife are problems."

"I should warn you, detective. I called the police, and they are on the way," Rose said.

"You're lying, Mrs. McClain. If someone were coming, I would have heard it by now on my radio. Besides, even if they are, you two will be dead."

As if it were on cue, the police radio blasted with a flurry of activity. A faint sound of sirens could be heard approaching. Then, chatter on his radio. "Entering the Walnut Street Inn now. Get backup here quick." Then, "We've got two people in custody. Heading down to the basement."

"Shit, Mrs. McClain. I wish you hadn't done that. It only

complicates matters."

"Shoot them, Jelks!" shouted Brandon Landers.

Brandon got within a few inches of Rose with his gun pointed at her head."

"Don't, Jelks. You're a cop. Don't kill an innocent person just because your medical bills are too high," Booger begged. "I can help you, too, you know."

"Jelks, shoot Mrs. McClain in the head!" Brandon Landers commanded.

Jelks's hand shook. Then he lowered his gun, turned, and said, "Listen, Landers, I took this job because I needed money for my wife's care. I took it to provide you police protection, not to kill anyone."

That's when Brandon fired three shots at the detective, and Jelks fell to the floor. Brandon then walked forward, looked Rose in her eyes, and shot her three times.

Rose fell to the floor. Her body was lifeless.

"No!" Booger screamed as he got up and prepared to leap at Brandon.

Just then, Jelks, not quite mortally wounded, turned slightly, pointed the gun, and shot Brandon Landers twice in the back. That would be the detective's last act before he took his final breath.

Booger fell to his wife's side and held her blood-soaked body in his arms as she clung to life.

"Baby, please don't leave me!" Booger cried.

Her limp and lifeless body looked like an angel to him. She was his whole world.

Suddenly, from the back of the room came a dozen or so armed men. Booger McClain was surrounded.

"I guess I'm in charge now," Pat said, pointing the gun at

Booger's head.

"You mean we're in charge," Ida said with a confident smile.

"Yes, dear," Pat replied.

Ida walked up to join Pat, gave him a kiss on the cheek, and pointed her gun directly at Booger.

It was just then that Randolph came running through the tunnel. Out of breath, he struggled to say, "There are at least a dozen policemen inside the inn. They've captured Sue Williams."

"It won't be long, and my dear wife will talk and lead them down here," Pat said.

"Plan B," Pat said as he turned to Ida and shot her directly in the head.

"It's time for us to get the Hell out of here," he said to the men behind him holding guns. "But first, I need to take care of you, McClain. You and your wife have been a real pain in the ass."

Just as Pat lifted his gun at Booger's head, eerie sounds came over the room, followed by weird-shaped shadows floating on the walls and floor, occupying the entire room. Everyone froze in place except Booger, who was too distraught to let go of his wife's hand.

"Ghosts," someone screamed.

Something frightening and beyond anyone's wildest imagination was happening in that room. Screams cried out. The bad guys tried to run, to escape, to get away from whatever was happening. But their bodies froze in place. No one in that room could move. Guns fell from everyone's hands, and they were powerless to retrieve them.

Dozens of shadows of creatures with man-like features, part animal, part man, completely covered the room. Then, the shadows became more pronounced and easier to identify, and finally, they materialized into man-animal creatures.

There was a man with a snake tail, a woman with a fish tail, half wolf, half man, part lion, part man, a man with a beak and wings, and a man who looked like a fire-breathing dragon. And there, standing over Rose and staring directly at Booger, was the man with a kangaroo tail. It was Samuel. He smiled and put out a hand, and Booger's tears suddenly dried, and a warm feeling came over the detective.

"A few friends of mine from the other side wanted to help."

Booger was in the presence of a host of angels.

"It's rare that I get visitors, but I think they've sensed my loneliness of late. Sometimes, the weight of evil can take its toll," Samuel said with the hint of a smile.

"Is it Rose's time?" the detective asked Samuel.

He said simply, "Yes."

"No!" Booger pleaded. "I just came back to her. Don't take her now. Let us have more time."

Then, another shadow appeared next to Samuel. When that shadow materialized, Booger recognized her. It was Mrs. Potts.

"Buford, I'm here to take Rose. Please do not be afraid. She is in good hands. She's going home, Buford."

"No, please, Mrs. Potts! It can't be her time. I came back for more than this. She needed me," he said with tears in his eyes, searching for answers. "We still have so much more to do. There are more lessons we can learn together. We can still help others. We will make the right choices of our free will, please. Mrs. Potts, please don't take my Rose. If you have to take someone, take me. I was supposed to go before her."

Before anyone could say anything else, Booger felt a touch on his hand, and he knew exactly what it was. Or, rather, who. It was Rose. He instantly felt a flood of unconditional love flow over him, and several moments flashed before his eyes as if projected onto the screen of his mind, though they were from her perspective.

First, he saw himself as he had been decades before at George's Steakhouse. After a night of working short-staffed, Rose had filled his coffee cup in a rush, and Booger said politely, "You know, your coffee is the best coffee in all of the Ozarks. I don't know how you do it, hun." Rose thanked him in an off-handed way, more concerned about getting tables cleaned off than anything else. Booger then left the restaurant, but not before leaving his customary $5 tip. It was the best tip she had received all night. They normally had more time to talk, but not that day. When Rose got back to the coffee pot, she realized it had been burning for hours and was now more like motor oil than coffee.

Next, Booger could see himself in Tahiti with Rose. He had had one too many Bahama Mamas by the pool when a young child hit an inflatable ball in his direction. Booger bent to pick it up, making polite conversation with the kid, when the detective's back seized him in a vice grip of pain before Booger gasped and then farted loudly for all nearby to hear. Booger then waddled back to the room, holding his hands near his butt to steady himself as Rose cackled with laughter.

The third image to flash before his eyes was from two weeks ago. Rose had run into the convenience store to get a drink, and as she was returning, she could see her husband clearly singing "Pink Pony Club" at the top of his voice with the windows rolled up. It had been a recent favorite of Rose's, but he had always acted unimpressed when it came on the radio.

She slowly returned to the passenger's side, and by the time she opened the door, he had George Straight playing. Rose smiled to herself and said nothing.

And that was it. She showed him a glimpse of her love, and then she was gone.

Happy tears rolled down Buford's face. He gently kissed his wife.

"Go on, Rose. It's okay. I'll be okay. Go on, dear. Go home."t.

Mrs. Potts, silent for a moment, then turned to Buford and said, "It is done. She has passed on." She shared with Booger a knowing glance, full of love, before she disappeared.

Then, the man-creatures, as if suddenly their work too was done, turned back into shadows and floated out of the room and out of sight.

After a moment of numb silence, Booger asked, "Who were those shadows, Samuel?".

"My family. After our encounter the other day, I recalled that I'd lost touch with the ones I care about most. In the end, the ones we love, the ones who truly know us and accept us, are everything. I invited them to join me tonight, and to my surprise, they all came."

Booger, numb to everything now, stood in disbelief for a minute before he said anything."Samuel, what am I to do? How can I bear this grief?"

"I can't answer that for you, friend. Take every day as if it is your last because when your last day comes, it comes now. Love with all your heart, right where you are, and always remember that you were left here to help others."

With that, Samuel returned to a shadow and disappeared.

The bad guys remained frozen in stunned silence right up

until dozens of policemen entered the room.

"What the hell has happened here, McClain?" a captain named Michael Moffitt asked.

"How did you know my name? I don't think we've met before."

"My dad told me all about you and described you down to a tee."

"Was your dad, Terrence Moffitt? The FBI agent?"

"Yes."

"My goodness. It's a small world."

"So, what happened here, McClain?"

"It's a long story, but in short, you need to arrest everyone here... They are all part of a drug and people trafficking ring. Look in this room, and there is another one down the tunnel. That will give you the evidence you need."

"Also, Moffitt, you should put out an APB for a school bus with 'College of the Ozarks' painted on its side and for a white passenger van with the Walnut Street Inn logo on its side. They both should be heading east on Highway 44, heading to St. Louis. That will give you all the evidence you need to put these people away for a long time."

CHAPTER TWENTY-FOUR
THE FUNERAL

Booger awoke around 6 AM the day of the funeral, laying in a bed for an extra minute, hoping beyond hope that the past four days had all been a dream. He then forced himself up to a chorus of bones popping – one in his right knee, one in his neck, and the other in his back. Every inch of him was sore and exhausted. Years of being blown up and shot down had taken their toll.

He started a pot of Folgers, which had tasted a lot like water recently, and grabbed the Sunday paper from the front door. After a quick shower, he headed to the office. He had a yellow legal pad where he had been writing a speech to give, and everything on it had been crossed out. All he wanted to do was lie back in his bed and die. Still, he knew he had to be strong for others. While the funeral service at White Chapel was going to be a small affair, he couldn't come with nothing to say, he thought. He wanted to honor Rose, but he didn't know how. He stared blankly at the legal pad for several minutes before throwing it in the trash.

At 11 AM, he arrived at the funeral home and cemetery near the airport. Booger had had his funeral and plot paid for for years. Always assuming he would die first, he didn't want Rose to have to worry about anything. He never thought he would be helping himself in a time of grief. "It should have been me," he whispered aloud as he awaited the family service counselor to meet with him and go over the final details.

The service in the chapel was larger than anticipated. All of the old staff from George's showed up to honor their friend, even though Booger had only reached out to Jessica, whom he knew Rose loved and cared for. He had also told her Facebook friends about the services, and well over 60 of them showed up – even two childhood pals from Arkansas. A couple of Rose's cousins also came. Then, Booger was pleased to see Joey and Billy Hoag from Hannibal. They were getting older now. And Lottie Creech came, too, flanked on each side by Megan Moxie and Betty Sue Dills. They brought condolences from the girls at Shadow Valley. Even the widow of Wichita detective Mason Chase and Millie Sanchez from Reeds Spring came. It was a sweet reminder of all the lives Rose touched. All of them took extra moments to talk to Booger, to hold his hand or give him hugs or pats on the back. Booger was not someone who liked others in his personal space, but he didn't mind it that day. In fact, he needed every touch and gesture.

An associate pastor from a small church in Republic, who was recommended by the funeral home staff, gave the blessings and did as well as anyone could expect. It was all a blur for Booger. He felt he was in a dream. "Is she really gone?" he wondered.

After the chapel service, two dozen or so people followed Booger and staff to the graveside, where a blue tent had been erected over the casket, next to folding chairs. The associate pastor gave another, more final blessing before turning to Booger to say a few words to those who had gathered to say their last goodbyes.

It was now time for Booger to speak.

"I didn't bring my notes today. They wouldn't have done me any good because I could never figure out what needed to be said, so I am going to have to wing this. First, I want you all to know that I really appreciate you showing up today for Rose. I have no doubt that she is smiling down on all of you. You have all been very kind to me, and your kindness is not wasted. I appreciate every word you've said – including your own, preacher," Booger said, nodding at the associate pastor, who kindly nodded back. "But words are just words. We give a lot of weight to them in times like these, but there are no words that can take away even an ounce of my grief. And there are no words that can bring my Rose back now, which is all I want in the world, so I don't see that good words are worth much. What you are left with here is raw emotion."

Booger stopped, needing to pause to keep from breaking down in tears. After a brief sniffle, he continued, "And while I am crippled with grief, I want you to know that that's not all I am. Because I am also overfilled with gratitude. I am so grateful for the time I had with my dear Rose. When you are young, you think you have all the time in the world, so you focus on selfish things. Those are different for everybody, but for me, I was focused on my career. First, I wanted to be a great cop, then a great FBI agent, and then a great private investigator. And as long as I felt like I was doing what I could in respect to my goals, then I was living my life right. But I am not young anymore, and I know better now. What really matters isn't what we achieve but who we help when help is needed and who helps us. I was lucky. And I still am because I had a few great moments in the sun with the women I loved, with my soulmate, Rose. She helped me, and I helped her. And together, we tried our best to help people in need. Standing before you now as a broken old man, I can tell you that that is the only thing that gives me any comfort. You did it, Rose," he said with tears streaming down his face, followed by a chuckle of laughter. "You didn't listen to me at all. You didn't stay safe in the car. God knows you would never do that. You followed me into a dark tunnel. And you helped stop the bad guys. You helped protect children who were being hurt by selfish people. And you did it by my side, teaching me in my old age what I should have learned years ago. You taught me what matters most. I love you, hun. Rest now. Rest now, my sweet Rose."

And with that, Booger collapsed next to the grave, bursting like a breached dam with tears. Several people ran to him, lifting him up, and for a few minutes, they all cried together.

After the service, Booger invited everyone back to his home for refreshments and drinks. Everyone had stories to share, and there was much laughter in between the poignant moments. Several people brought casseroles, for which the detective was grateful. He hadn't eaten well in days and suddenly felt famished. Booger tried them all before lifting the napkin over a basket of danishes left by his old friends, the Browns, who had stepped out quietly, unseen. Booger recognized the taste immediately. It was kale and spinach. The detective smiled to himself and said nothing.

THE END

Alan Brown grew up in the suburbs of Kansas City and graduated from Shawnee Mission East High School in 1973 and Avila University in 1979. Now He lives in a suburb of St. Louis, MO, with my wife and three daughters. He also has four sons who are grown and living outside the home. He enjoys writing about experiences he had growing up, examining the fantastical side, the dark side of a person's natural fears. All of his books are based on a reality in his life. He is a fan of Alfred Hitchcock. Like his stories, Alan Brown's will conclude with a twist, something he hopes will take the reader by surprise.

Brian Brown - I am a husband, father of four, and a former business and political reporter from Springfield, Missouri, who currently lives and works in the St. Louis area. I've written five books with my father, Alan Brown, and edited a sixth. All our novels involve our fictional detective, Booger McClain, in what we have dubbed our Ozarks' Noir style. I'm also an amateur photographer: @Bbrownspfd on Instagram. More information about our novels is available on our Facebook page (Alan and Brian Brown Write Stuff): https://www.facebook.com/profile. php?id=100064104282706